THE LOQUAT EYES

THE LOQUAT EYES

MORE TALL TALES FROM COTTON COUNTY, TEXAS

by

Ardath Mayhar

THE BORGO PRESS

An Imprint of Wildside Press LLC

MMX

CONTENTS

TWO CHILDREN'S FANTASIES

PROLOGUE

Some decades ago I wrote a book of East Texas tales that was published under the title, *Slewfoot Sally and the Flying Mule*. The narrator, in that work, was actually my own father, a great storyteller, who was disguised as Solomon Peat. Even after I finished the book and went on to other projects, I kept hearing Dad's voice telling me more stories, some of them of actual happenings, some that others had told to me in the past. So here is an additional group of Uncle Sol's stories that had been waiting for a chance to be heard.

Along with these I've included two children's fantasies, "The Jeweled Mouse" and "The Kingdom of Yip," which seemed to fit well with these tall tales from Cotton County, Texas.

—Ardath Mayhar
Chireno, Texas
November, 2009

*My thanks to my schoolmate Charles Shadden for telling
me this story, which really happened.*

THE DAY OF THE BOOMERS

Solomon Peat trudged along the dirt road toward Mrs.
Bragg's store, his cousin Willa's protests still ringing in
his ears. "You're too old to walk that far, Sol! You got a
perfectly good Ford there in the garage, and it just sits
there unless I take it in to Tompkins when I go shopping."

He snorted dust out of his nose as the bread truck
passed him, going back to town. As usual, Mrs. Bragg had
probably cussed Tim Banks out for being late, though it
was actually a bit earlier than usual. If that woman
couldn't find something to fuss about, she was plumb miserable, he thought.

His knees began to pop and creak, but by now the store
was in sight, its tin roof shining through the trees beyond
the bend in the road leading to Possum Creek. Since he retired a while back, his daily trip to the store had been just
about his only recreation. His eyes had got too bad for
reading much and he never had been one for dominos.

He had his eye on some boys who also liked to fre-
quent the store. Will Henry was his great-nephew, and

Chuck was shirt-tail kin, as well. Tim and Les and Fane lived close by and came to the store for their mama, though the younger two were a bit too small to sit still for a good story. The bigger boys were coming along fine, though, always ready to sit down with a strawberry pop in hand (otherwise Mrs. Bragg considered them nuisances instead of customers) and listen as he spun his tales.

It was early summer, and the boys were already sitting in the shade of the chinaberry tree beside the store. Dust rose about them as they scuffled like a pile of pups, and he grinned, remembering the time, a half century or more ago, when he had done the same with his own brothers. Will Henry looked up and yelled a greeting, and Sol raised his hat and wiped sweat from his flushed forehead. By the time he climbed the porch steps, the five were lined up like blackbirds on a limb, waiting for him.

He dropped into his hickory splint chair, panting a bit, and dug into the pocket of his hickory striped overalls for change. "Go buy you some pop," he grunted. "Then come back out and talk."

At that moment, there was a distant roar that grew louder and louder as a jet plane zoomed low over the swamp country, ripping across the sky as if to tear off your scalp. Sol began to grin. "Got a tale to tell you about the day the boomers come over Tompkins, during the war."

"Boomers?" Will Henry was already hooked, it was clear, for he scampered into the store clutching his quarter and was out again before Chuck and the other boys had time to get in the door. "What are boomers?" he asked. "And which war?"

"You just wait," Sol told him.

When the five boys, two white and three black, were

lined up along the edge of the porch, Sol leaned the back of his chair against the wall of the store and looked off across the woods. "You studied about the Second World War yet in school?" he asked.

Will Henry nodded. Chuck grimaced, and Tim, a year younger, did, too. Les and Fane were watching a grand-daddy longlegs climb the porch post and paid no attention. Most of the time the little fellows were engaged in some strange communication of their own, anyway, that involved grins and snickers and occasional nudges with elbows.

"Well," Sol said, settling his hands on his knees and his head back against the wall, "Back when I was just too old to get into the fun, we fought a big war with Germany and Japan, and that was World War Two. There was a lot of fighting overseas, and planes flew over and dropped bombs on cities on both sides. Nasty bus'ness.

"Out here in the river bottoms, the old folks never heard the word bomber, so they said boomer when the subject come up, which was pretty often, about then, because the newspapers were always talking about 'em. One day there was a big ruckus about air-raid drills. The paper said a boomer was goin' to fly over all of East Texas and take pictures of the downtown streets to see how well we could do if we got attacked.

"There'd be a siren go off, and that meant everybody was to get inside and stay quiet. Course, I never did figure out how that would do you a bit of good, if that boomer had dropped a bomb right spang on top of you, but gov'ment folks seem to have to play that kind of game, now and again.

"Anyway, they was s'posed to take them pictures and

print 'em in each town's newspapers. It was s'posed to make us all feel patriotic, I think, though I thought at the time it was kind of silly."

He thumped the legs of his chair down onto the porch and held out a quarter to Will Henry. "You go and get me a strawberry pop, Will? I'm workin' up a thirst, here."

After the first long sip, he leaned back again and went on. "They picked a Saturday to do that, and my Daddy, who was old fashioned as they come, had come to town in his wagon, behind his team of blue mules that he was proud of as all get-out. He stopped at the drugstore on his way to my house and hitched them to the post there before he went inside to get some medicine for Gramma.

"I was there already, drinkin' a milk shake, and he found a lot of other folks he knowed there, most of 'em pretty old because the young folks had mostly gone off to the army or to the Coast to build ships and such.

"Anyway, while he was talkin' away, that siren went off. Like to of scared us all to death, but we was doing pretty well until Miss Mattie Nokes's little terrier jumped out of her arms and took off toward the mules, barkin' fit to drive 'em out of their minds. That siren had made 'em skittish, already.

"Sal, the lead mule, jerked her hitch loose and Lucy, the off mule, did the same, and they took off up the street as fast as they could go, with the wagon bouncin' and jan-glin' behind 'em. After them went that damn dog, and af-ter it come Miss Mattie, all red faced and yellin' at the top of her lungs. Course, soon as he seen what happened, the constable started off after the whole shebang, and the Misses Penton stuck their heads out of the dress shop and then run along, too, with their hair-buns floppin' loose on the tops of their heads.

"I was running after Daddy, who was right behind the constable, when I heard a plane comin' over low. I ducked my head and kept goin', because I wanted to make sure Daddy was all right. When I glanced back, I could see a whole street-full of folks streamin' along behind us, just tearin' out like it was a road race instead of an air raid alarm.

"I guess the folks in that plane wondered what had gone wrong when they passed over and taken their pictures.

"Nobody ever printed any picture of Tompkins's drill, that was for sure, though every other little town around here had a shot of empty streets on the front pages of their papers.

"I wondered for years and years how it looked, and when I started to manage the sawmill I got to know Miz Helen, the newspaper lady. I finally talked her into showin' me that picture, and it was a doozie. I could tell just who everybody was—recognized every last one of them, down to that dratted terrier.

"Way back at the end of the bunch come Gimpy Harrell on his go-cart, pushin' himself along with both hands. I was the only one in the whole entire batch you couldn't identify, because I had my head ducked down.

"I was pretty glad I'd done that when I saw it, because poor Daddy looked mad enough to chew railroad spikes. His mouth was wide open, and I knew what sort of language he'd been yellin' at them mules. No wonder they looked kind of wilted, up there leadin' the parade."

He sighed and took a long pull at his pop. "I wish now I'd have paid to have her make me a copy of that thing, though she'd have been lynched if anybody suspected she did it. Folks around here was ashamed of that for years and years. Said if it'd been a real war, we'd of been blowed sky high, every last one of us." He drained the bottle and set it neatly in the empty soda-water case that sat beside his chair.

"But I figured if the boomers could find our town, what difference did it make whether anybody was out on the street? We'd have been just as dead hidin' in the drugstore or behind the harness racks in Wilder's hardware or in a toilet paper box behind the cafe. Bombs, the way I see it, don't care whether you know they're comin' or not."

Will Henry drew a long breath around the neck of his bottle. "Did your daddy catch his mules?" he asked, always practical.

"They stopped just outside town at the foot of Long Hill. They was just plain tuckered out with all the excitement. Everybody blamed them for the mess, too, which wasn't a bit fair. It was Miss Mattie's nasty little Nicky-Poo that caused all the trouble."

The door opened and Mrs. Bragg tramped heavily across the porch to her own sag-bottomed chair. "I recall that, too, Sol. I was in Tompkins for my aunt's birthday, and seemed as if everybody talked about the stampede most of that week. 1943, that was? Yes, I think so. Not one of the better years." She fanned herself with the corner of her apron and looked up the road.

"I wonder when the catfish man will get here. I got customers waitin' for fish, and that crazy idiot thinks he's got to stop and gossip with everybody along the way. Time he gets here, my fish'll be turned, you just watch and see." She rose and thudded back into the store.

Solomon looked at Will, who looked at Chuck, who pinched Tim, who nudged Les, who passed it on to Fane. They all knew Mrs. Bragg better than she realized.

She'd have been flat disappointed if the catfish man came on time.

"Boomers," Will Henry murmured, his eyes fixed on some inner vision.

Les and Fane dissolved into giggles as Les held the daddy longlegs by his hind legs and made him point the way home with his front four. Of course if they'd followed directions, they'd have had to go three different ways, but that didn't spoil the fun at all.

Chuck, in his usual deliberate way, was working himself through the story, bit by bit. At last he had the vision firmly in mind. He began to grin.

Solomon watched him, his own eyes half closed, as he began to go pink and to shake. Then Sol's booming laugh joined the boy's, and the rest of the crew began to laugh, too.

Disgrace or not, that had to have been one of the funniest things Tompkins, Texas, had ever seen in its staid and dusty streets.

Again, Charles Shadden was on the spot and saw the incident that worked itself into this tale.

NOT A PRETTY SIGHT

It was mid-morning, and Possum Creek (what there was of it) dozed in the June heat. Uncle Sol Peat's cadre of boys, usually more than ready for a story, had gone fishing, leaving the old fellow sitting on the porch of Mrs. Bragg's grocery store, half dozing, with his chair cocked back against the wall and his head drooped over sideways.

All the salesmen had come and gone early, because the weekend was coming up and little country stores always ran out of bread and soft drinks and such over Friday and Saturday. There wasn't even a stray customer to waylay with a tale so intriguing that nobody could walk away and leave it unfinished.

Mrs. Bragg had been putting up stock since daylight, and now she came thumping out onto the porch and sat in her sag-seated chair to cool off. "Wake up, Sol! You been asleep all mornin'. I want to ask you if you remember somebody, which I know is ridiculous. You remember everybody and everything that ever crossed the road or sat under a tree."

He opened one pale blue eye, the exact shade of his washed-out denim overalls, and sighed. "What you need to know?" he asked, his tone as mild as possible. It didn't do to go at Mrs. Bragg too brashly, for she had a tongue that could strip the bark off a hickory tree.

"You recall that woman who ran the beauty shop in Templeton, back about thirty years ago? Right on the corner of the main road and Sassafrass Street, it was. She was a cousin of my mother's on her daddy's side. I just got word last night that she died Monday night. Had a stroke. Too bad—she used to do a mighty fine job of setting hair."

Sol thumped his chair legs onto the floor and sat straight. "Allie Johnson. I do remember her. My wife used to go to her shop, back when I was runnin' the mill in Templeton. My Lord, that's a long time ago. Nearer forty years than thirty."

He stared at Mrs. Bragg, and his round belly began to joggle. In a bit the rest of him joined in, which was an infallible sign that a funny story was on its way.

"Now what?" she asked in a mordant tone, though her expression belied it. Mrs. Bragg, deny it how she might, loved Solomon's stories as much as any of the small boys, traveling salesmen, or random customers who visited her store.

Sol wiped his eyes on a spotless handkerchief and said, "Did you ever know old Bonaparte Collum? Lived in the boarding house at the corner of Sassafrass and Pecan, couple of blocks down from the beauty parlor. Skinniest old fellow you ever saw in your life."

Mrs. Bragg looked thoughtful. "Now you mention it, I seem to recall an old fellow, thin as a rail, wore a long-tailed black coat and stovepipe britches; he used to walk over to the big grocery store every day. What is it about him...? I seem to recall he did something really awful. Got the reputation of being a dirty old man, way back before anybody invented the term."

Sol began to laugh again, helplessly, and she had to wait until he simmered down to ask, "Now what on earth do you know about him?"

"How he got that reputation—which he never in any way deserved or did anything to earn." Again Sol wiped his eyes and settled his feet firmly on the porch.

"Old Boney was the sweetest old fellow you ever met in your life. Always a cheerful word, never a step out of the straight and narrow. At least, as long as I knowed him, which was some twenty years. Might be, he kicked up his heels a bit when he was young, but that had to have been about the time Noah was building his boat."

"Then why in tarnation did all the ladies in Templeton think he was the devil incarnate?" Mrs. Bragg asked. Her elbows were on her knees now, her chin stuck out at the angle that warned of coming conflict.

"Because of Miss Mattie Nokes's nasty little terrier, Nicky-Poo."

"Why, I remember that little dog. Friendly little thing, just would wag that tail of hers at everybody. You can't tell me a sweet little dog could ruin a man's reputation that way!" The chin came out another fraction of an inch.

"That was the meanest animal God ever put fur on," Uncle Sol said. He spat tobacco juice neatly into his snuff can and put the lid on, wiped his lips, and drew his cottony eyebrows down into a V over his pudgy nose. "Nicky-Poo would bite anybody that couldn't afford to fight back. Little kids, men who couldn't lower themselves to kick a dog the size of a loaf of bread, and old fellows like Boney, though he didn't know that in time to save himself."

"Tell," said Mrs. Bragg, folding her arms over her impressive bosom and staring at Sol as if in challenge.

Sol leaned himself comfortably into the back of his chair and looked off over the pine trees as if bringing a vision of the past to life. "That was in the Thirties, before anyplace had air conditioning, you remember? That big old house on the corner had been cut up into apartments, and the corner of the ground floor was the beauty shop.

"Miss Mattie had an apartment right next to it, as I recall, and she used to let Nicky-Poo out to do her...to run around and get her exercise. She would get through with her serious affairs and lie down on the sidewalk right in front of the beauty parlor to catch forty winks.

"My wife used to tell me that Hell wasn't a bit hotter than that beauty shop in summer. What with the hot water and the dryers and the other stuff making for even more heat, the ladies just simply couldn't stand it unless they taken off their dresses."

Mrs. Bragg looked shocked, but her lip began to twitch. "I do remember that. Just down to our slips, which was about as modest as anybody ever gets, these days. Back then, though, it was right next to sinful. But, Lord, no man would have thought of going into a beauty shop, then, any more than they'd go buy underwear for their wives. We were safe from any outsider."

"Yes, that's what they thought. Until Nicky-Poo took a hand—or a tooth, I ought to say—in the business.

"Now you've got to realize that I wasn't eavesdroppin'. I'd wrenched my back moving some equipment at the mill, and I was propped up in a chair over at Dr. Tatum's office, waiting for a chiropractic treatment. Couldn't move to do any good at all, but I could watch what was goin' on out in Sassafrass Street, which was precious little." He sighed and shifted his weight, as if that old pain still bothered him.

"There was Nicky-Poo, lying on the sidewalk, looking sound asleep, though I figured that was just her sneaky way of gettin' a victim within reach of her nasty little teeth. And there was Boney, tottering along on his skinny legs, held up by his walking stick. Most every day he went to the store to get him a cold drink, and it was a wonder he ever made it, he was so wavery on his pins.

"I saw him heading toward Nicky-Poo, and if I could have got up I'd have run to warn him, but I was stuck like a bug in a jug, and he was so deaf he'd never have heard a yell. He got closer and closer, and I could see an ear twitch just a little, as that dog gauged her distance.

"I was about to call for the doctor to run and warn him when that terrier moved like a bolt of lightning. She came up, caught that poor old man's skinny shank in her teeth, and hung on like grim death.

"Boney screamed to wake the dead and tried to beat her off with his walkin' stick, but she hung on like a snappin' turtle, and he couldn't budge her. He looked around kind of wild and big-eyed, and spotted the door to the beauty shop, though I doubt he even knew what it was, he was so old fashioned and out of it. Anyway, he scooted up the steps onto that high veranda and into the door before I could prepare myself for what had to happen."

Mrs. Bragg was sitting straight now, her own eyes a bit large, listening intently. From time to time she nodded, as if recognizing something familiar.

"I never heard such a commotion, not even when I was in the Army. Shouts and screams and bangs and thuds—it seemed as if Armageddon had come, right there in that beauty parlor. I could hear a wild sort of yell that I figured came out of Boney, being as the ladies were shriller, and the poor old fellow come boltin' out of the door, running. Absolutely running, though he could hardly walk, in the ordinary way."

Sol folded his hands over his paunch and stared straight into Mrs. Bragg's eyes. "He dashed across that veranda and off the edge above the steps, straight out into the air as if he was flyin'. Legs pumpin', arms wavin', coattails flappin', he just sailed out into space...and went smush onto that new cement sidewalk.

"Of course, Nicky-Poo took off as soon as he hit the steps goin' in, so nobody had a clue she was involved at all. Out of the shop boiled about a dozen ladies, forgettin' entirely that they was dressed only in their slips and corsets and other underwear, which a gentleman don't inquire about too close.

"They swarmed down the steps and begun beatin' that old man with purses and umbrellas and towels and anything else they could catch up on the way out. He was squirmin' and moanin' and they was yelling all sorts of things, none of which sounded too ladylike to me, but I admit I was a mite far off to hear exactly what was said.

"By then the chiropractor was leanin' out his window beside me, and the other patients had took notice, but I was the onliest one who saw the whole entire thing from beginnin' to end. When the ambulance pulled up, the doctor went out to see could he help, and when he come back he said the old man had all sorts of broke bones. But the ladies was all still fussin' about perverts and dirty old men and such, so they didn't pay much mind to how bad he was hurt."

"How bad was he hurt?" Mrs. Bragg inquired.

"Broke both legs, one hip, and dislocated his jaw. That, I think, must have been Mrs. Hillcock's big purse, that they used to swear she loaded with bricks before she left home. I saw her hit him upside the head with it. Old fellow was crippled the rest of his life. Which, maybe, was best, for he never had to walk past Nicky-Poo again."

"You mean, all those years, he was innocent?" Mrs. Bragg asked, her voice filled with shock and disappointment.

"The onliest guilty party was Mattie Nokes's Nicky-Poo, and she was never suspected for a minute. Even though I sent my wife over to the shop, when she come after me, to give Mrs. Johnson the straight of the story. She just pooh-poohed the whole idea. Seems, somehow, I had the reputation for stretchin' things a mite, even way back then."

Mrs. Bragg stretched out her feet, leaned back in her chair, and let loose with the deepest laugh she had given in years. Uncle Sol began to joggle again, and the two of them sent waves of laughter ringing over the pine trees and into the summer sky.

When they finished, Mrs. Bragg rose, gathered her dignity about her like a queen's robe, and stalked into the store again. Sol shook his head, wondering if she'd ever admit having laughed at one of his stories.

Probably not, he decided.

This tale has its origin in the fact that my own grand-mother had chronic catarrh. My grandfather, who was station agent for Santa Fe Railroad in Timpson, Texas, ex-changed homes and jobs for one year with the agent in West Texas. After that year, my grandmother was cured of her ailment.

ON LOAN TO COUSIN SARAH

Solomon Peat had leaned his hickory splint chair at a perilous angle against the front wall of Mrs. Bragg's store. The pale dust of the road gleamed almost gold in the bright sunshine, but a breeze found its way, from time to time, through the surrounding pine forest. In the shade of the porch and its adjacent chinaberry tree, Sol found it tolerably cool.

It was also lonesome. Mrs. Bragg was inside the store, checking her stock and enjoying the electric fan she had bought new this summer. It was too hot for many customers to venture out after bread or milk or cold drinks, and the porch had been empty for an hour.

Sol needed an audience to be perfectly happy. He was just about to wander up the road toward his own home and a nap when Will Henry and Chuck came into view, their bicycle wheels leaving a thin trail of dust in the air behind them.

They arrived, their faces scarlet with heat and effort, and Sol handed out quarters for strawberry pop before they had a chance to mention the need. Grinning, they scooted into the store and returned with damp red bottles beginning to frost in the humid air.

"Glad to see you boys. What you been doin' this morning?" Sol asked. "I'd have thought it was too hot for your mamas to put you to work."

"Not our mamas," Will Henry muttered around the neck of his pop bottle. "Our Aunt Jenny. We got loaned out, and that's worse than workin' for our own folks."

Chuck drew a deep breath and heaved a sigh. "Aunt Jenny had to go to Templeton, and we had to *baby-sit*. I'd rather work in the garden or even *mow grass*. Those kids of hers can outrun a rabbit and out-fox a fox. Kept us hoppin' all morning."

Will Henry wiped his strawberry colored lips on his cotton sleeve and stared up at Uncle Sol. "You ever baby-sit?" he asked. "I hate it, myself."

Solomon began to chuckle. His round stomach joggled like a bowl of Jell-O, and his blue eyes disappeared into the creases formed by his fat cheeks and his overhanging eyebrows. "Have I ever baby-sat? Boys, I got loaned out on the longest baby-sitting job you ever could've dreamed up."

Both boys sat up straight, their faces filled with interest, while Sol spat his tobacco chew neatly into his snuff can and settled his chair into tale-telling position against the gray wood of the wall. His pale blue eyes took on a distant look, as they always did when he looked into the past.

"I was about nine or thereabouts at the time, which is a tad younger than either of you boys. Still, I thought I was growed up entirely. Pa let me plow by myself, and even Ma depended on me to chop most of the firewood for the kitchen stove, though my big brother Yale still cut the big logs for the fireplace.

"School was out for the summer and the crop was laid by when Mama's Cousin Sarah come visitin'. Sarah was a long, tall, sad-lookin' woman with two little girls and a new baby. I didn't know it at the time, but she had come on purpose to borrow me from Mama, because she was having so much trouble with her catarrh."

"What's catarrh?" Chuck asked, always interested in anything he didn't understand.

"That's what they used to call sinus trouble, when your nose either ran like a river or stopped up and you had terrible headaches. Mostly it came and went, but with Cousin Sarah it came and stayed till her husband Willie Earl decided to do somethin' about it.

"Willie was station agent at Templeton for the H.E. & W.T. railroad. He was a good one, too, and the company listened when he asked them if he could swap jobs and houses and furniture for a year with a fellow who worked the station at Haskell, out in West Texas. The doctor said the drier climate might help Sarah, and he was willing to try it.

"That man seemed to think it'd be nice to have a change of scenery for his family, so he agreed to do it, too. So the whole entire family, including their milk cow, was about to get into a boxcar with what they'd need for a year and go west, and they needed help doin' it."

Will Henry was looking impressed, and it took a lot to achieve that. "They just got in the boxcar and took off? That's kind of neat," he said.

"Would've been if I'd just heard about it, but I had to go along and help DO it, and that was a lot of work. Being summer, it was hot as the toenails of hell, too, and riding in the same space with a cow means you ride along with her manure, as well. It was one of my jobs to shovel the messy straw out along the right-of-way as we traveled, which wasn't my favorite part of the trip, I can tell you."

Mrs. Bragg appeared on the porch, carrying her bottle of grape soda, and dropped into the other hickory splint chair. "Too hot in there," she complained, but Sol grinned, for he knew she had never heard this particular tale. He hadn't thought about this one in years and years.

"Anyway, we rode and rode, and about the middle of the second day we stopped and there was Haskell, which wasn't a good hole in the road. We manhandled that cow off the train and unloaded the trunks of clothes and pots and pans and home canned stuff into a wagon.

"We wound up at a frame house that looked as if it had been sand-blasted, the paint was so wore down. I learned the hard way that it had—the wind never stopped blowin', seemed as if, and that gritty sand worked its way into the house under doors, around windows. You just couldn't keep it out. I'd find it between my teeth when I woke up in the mornin' and in my plate at meals. It was a bother."

"Were there any more kids to play with besides your little girl cousins and the baby?" Chuck asked. "It'd be almighty lonesome out there with nobody you knew from school."

"Didn't have time to be lonesome," Sol said. "It kept

us busy from dawn to dark tendin' to the little 'uns and sweepin' out that dratted dust. Willie Earl went to work at seven in the mornin' and stayed there till midnight. I'd take him a lunch down to the station about noon, but he wouldn't stop till quittin' time."

Sol grinned suddenly. "Old Willie Earl was a funny person. He'd tackle a bear and give it the first two bites, but he was mortally afraid of a dead body. One come in one evening around nine o'clock and had to wait there until the five-o'clock express come through the next mornin'. Willie woke me up out of a sound sleep to come down and set with him till his shift was over.

"I'll never forget settin' there on that long, hard bench in the waiting room, hearin' the telegraph clicking off and on. That long box in the freight room seemed like it fascinated Willie, for he'd go back and check on it every so often, and I could feel that dead man in it, as if he was tryin' to tell us somethin'. That was likely the longest three hours I ever spent in my life, I tell you." He sighed and rose to buy a bottle of pop for himself, for storytelling dried him out considerably.

When he settled back again, he continued, "Bein' summer, there wasn't any school, and nobody lived on the little dead-end street with us except the Vinceys, right across the way. Miz Vincey was what they used to call socially prominent, and that house was the only one in town that was painted every year. It had a curved porch round the front and a cupola on top and fancy gingerbread trim that must have been a problem to paint.

"Time passed, and Cousin Sarah was poorly for a long while. School started, and there were other children to play with, which kept me and the girls occupied all winter.

Then came spring again, and I was missin' my family something terrible. I knowed Cousin Sarah was lonesome, too, though she was gettin' better all the time.

"At first she thought it'd be nice to have another lady so close to visit with, but once Miz Vincey's baby came, that spring, she changed her mind in a hurry. You see, Cousin Sarah, just like Mama, was so clean it hurt. That was why we kept battlin' that dust all the time." He sneezed three times, very quickly, as if that long-ago dust still haunted him.

"It's funny—even with the dust, Cousin Sarah got well. Never sneezed, never had those nasty headaches, didn't snort and blow all night. She even felt like goin' to church and such, and about the time she was ready to make a friend of Miz Vincey, that baby came. What happened then put her off that woman like a dirty pair of drawers."

Mrs. Bragg frowned down her nose. "Now, Sol, no need to be vulgar," she said in her most disapproving tone.

"True, though. You see, that big house had a fancy big storm cellar beside the kitchen door, which was on the side of the house rather than at the back. It had a stovepipe to let in air and double doors that opened out like wings.

"Tornados were bad in that area, so most places had a hole you could duck into if you needed to, but that was one big cellar. Once the baby was born, Cousin Sarah went over to visit and took Miz Vincey an embroidered bib and some other stuff. She come back red as a beet and told us not to let her hear of our goin' over there.

"No telling what you'd catch," she said to me and her girls. "That woman is filthy and slack-twisted to boot."

She wouldn't say what set her off so bad. At least not

to us youngsters. But she used to wait up for Willie Earl, when she was upset about somethin', and I figured she was plenty upset that night, so I hid in the pantry until Willie got home. Sure enough, Sarah waited up, too, and had him fresh coffee and a snack waitin' when he got there.

"He hadn't got set down good when she started tellin' him about Miz Vincey. And as she talked I got to feel like she did. No tellin' WHAT you'd catch over there.

"'While I was THERE, William,' Sarah said, 'She changed that baby twice. She took those dirty diapers—and they were DIRTY—and flung them out the door into that storm cellar.

"'I asked her if she wanted to know how I kept Bessie's diapers so clean, but she shook her head. 'I'll just throw them in till it fills up, then I'll get Evalina to come and boil out the whole bunch,' she told me."

"I have to admit that the idea made even me a bit sick, not to mention thinking about what poor old Evalina, who did odd jobs for ladies all over town, had to go through. I watched and waited, when Sarah gave me the time, to see how long Miz Vincey could go before she had to wash up those filthy diapers.

"It got so I was kind of fascinated by that open storm cellar—you could smell it, if the wind was right, clear over to our house, and I hated to think what Mr. Vincey had to smell while he ate supper with the kitchen door open. But maybe they got so used to the stink they never noticed it. Anyway, it took two months for the thing to fill clear up."

Mrs. Bragg was looking pained. "Think of the filth!" she groaned. "Think of the maggots—and worse—that had to be growing in that mess. And that poor baby! How could they ever get those didies clean enough not to irritate his little bottom?"

"Well, I wondered the same thing, having had dealings with little Bessie's diaper situation. I'd put cornstarch in her diapers, like Sarah taught me, to keep her from gettin' diaper rash, and I felt a kind of professional interest in what would happen to pore little old Jimmy across the road.

"However, Cousin Sarah wouldn't go over there again for any reason, and she kept an eye on us to keep us from even crossin' the road.

"When Evalina kindled a big fire under the wash pot behind the Vincey house, I made up errands to run that would take me far enough up the street to see what she was doing. She used a lot of lye, believe me, and she boiled pots and pots of wash, dumped the water, boiled 'em again, and I guess she finally got 'em clean.

"About that time the year was up, and Willie Earl was ready to go home. We packed up everything again, including the cow, and got on another boxcar and headed for Templeton. I never found out if those didies killed that baby or not.

"Mama was just about sick when I told her about that. She wrote Cousin Sarah to make sure I wasn't makin' up stories, and when Sarah's letter came she apologized for doubtin' my word." Sol shook his head gravely at Mrs. Bragg.

"Seems as if even the thought of babysitting or storm cellars can bring back that smell...." He turned to the boys, who had finished their strawberry pop. "I need another one to take the taste out of my mouth. You boys game?"

When Chuck and Will Henry went into the store to

fish in the deep cooler of icy water, Mrs. Bragg turned her stony gaze on Sol. "You sure that really happened, Solomon?" she asked.

"I hate to say it, but it's Gospel," he said. "Mama and Cousin Sarah put their heads together and had fits about the situation as long as they lived. And even now, I wonder if that poor baby survived."

The boys were back by then, dripping bottles in hand, and Sol took a deep swallow and belched gently. "So don't think any old baby-sittin' job is bad until you run into one that's got a lot of bells and whistles attached."

They sat on the edge of the porch and nodded, looking thoughtful. Seemed as if nothing they did could top the things that had happened to Uncle Solomon Peat in the course of his long and active life.

We owned that bantam hen, and I once saw her attack a hawk with my own eyes. It was an amazing thing to see, as she flew up and battered the predator until he dropped her chick. She also raised a hatching of quail.

FIERCE AS A BANTY HEN

Mrs. Bragg had a soft spot, though Solomon Peat had always known that nobody else actually realized it. He'd known her for decades, and in all that time he'd only known her to let her closely hidden charities show twice. The first time was so long ago he couldn't remember what it had been, but now, sitting on the front porch of the small store, he was watching the result of the second one peck and scratch about the dust under the chinaberry tree.

The storekeeper had let old Aunt Tildy trade her a bantam hen and chicks to square away her recently dead daughter's grocery bill. There wasn't much way you could hide a bantam hen.

The small gray-brown creature was busy scratching up new food supplies for her six chicks, making the dirt fly and from time to time settling onto her chest to dust-clean her feathers. She was interrupted by the arrival of two small boys. Chuck and Will Henry pedaled their bikes into the shade and leaned them against the chinaberry without so much as an apology to the ruffled bantam.

The sun was high, and heat hung over the piney woods like a thick blanket. Sol dug into his overalls pocket and held out quarters to Will Henry, then to Chuck. Before they got into the store, three small figures appeared down the road to the river, and Sol began to dig again. This morning, it seemed, he'd have his full complement of listeners, for a while.

When the three black boys and two white ones were settled along the edge of the porch, sipping from frosty red bottles, Sol cocked his chair back against the wall and cleared his throat. Six brown eyes, two gray ones, and two blue ones focused on him expectantly.

"See that banty hen out there?" he asked, pointing toward the small family under the tree. "You'll never see anything braver than a banty hen, I guarantee it. Once when I was a boy Ma's sister gave her bantam hen and rooster. The little hen hatched six chicks out in the brush, but soon as they could get around she brought 'em to the house. Ma was proud as punch of 'em."

Will Henry squirmed impatiently. He'd seen entirely too many chickens that morning, helping his mama clean out the poultry yard. A squingy little thing like that hen wasn't something that interested him.

Sol, understanding the boy better than Will Henry understood himself, spat tobacco juice into the snuff can he kept for that purpose and leaned back even more comfortably. "One mornin' I was cutting the grass along the back fence when a hawk swooped down and grabbed one of her chicks, almost right under my nose.

"I was about to run after the .22, but before I could

move, that crazy little critter flew up twenty feet in the air and began beatin' that hawk with her wings and clawing him with her feet till he had to drop her chick and fly for his life. The chick came down fine—bantams are light enough to fly pretty good, and he was almost half growed by then.

"That banty landed beside him, shooed him back to the rest of the bunch, and went right on scratchin' up worms. When I had time to consider that the hawk was about five times her size, I decided that was a gutsy thing to do. But that wasn't the last adventure that hen had."

Will Henry, confronted with an irrefutably heroic act, had settled in to listen, as Sol intended for him to do. The old man nodded and went on, "My Pa might work like a mule at makin' crops, but he dearly loved to hunt bobwhite quail. He never bothered a nest if he could help it, and he wouldn't allow town fellows to hunt on our farm. That was reserved for him and my uncles.

"One summer Pa was drivin' the hay mower along, not thinkin' about anything much, and the mule went right over a quail nest close to the corner of the hayfield. The hen quail darted off, and Pa knew she'd never come back to her nest. They don't, you know, once they're disturbed.

"Pa, he whoa'd the mule and got down off the iron seat of the mower. He gathered up the eggs and put 'em in the shade by the fence. When he got through he took 'em to the house in his hat and gave 'em to Ma. That was maybe two years after she got the banties, and that first hen was settin' on a bunch of eggs, right then.

"Ma took the eggs out from under her and put 'em under another one that was setting. Then she put the quail eggs in a nest in her covered pen where she usually put new-hatched chicks and set that little hen on 'em." He looked down at the five intent faces.

"You ever seen a quail egg?" he asked. Only Tim admitted to having had that pleasure, so he went on, "They're about the size of the end of your little finger, round on one end, kind of pointy on the other. She settled on those eggs as nice as you please, and for a while we just fed and watered her and didn't think much about it.

"One morning I went out to feed the hen and that little pen, which had a chick-wire top over it, was just full of tiny little quail. They looked just exactly like baby banties, though about half the size, and they was flyin' up and bouncin' off the wire. They hatch able to fly, seems as if.

"I bent over and looked under the shelter, and there was all the eggshells, lookin' just like somebody had opened the round end with a can opener, leavin' the tops hinged back, just as neat. And that hen was just as happy as if those was her own children. When we let 'em all out, she led the bunch around just like that one out there is doin', huntin' out bugs and such. Course, out of the ten, four took off pretty quick and joined up with the covey of quail just over the fence from the vegetable garden. Still, that left six, which kept that banty pretty d...darn busy."

Mrs. Bragg had come out on the porch and dropped into her own hickory splint chair, which was shaped exactly like her substantial rear end. "Never heard this tale before, Sol," she said.

Not often did the storekeeper admit any interest in his stories, but Uncle Sol pretended not to notice. Instead, he went on, "You boys know how quail roost at night, don't you?"

This time there was a chorus of, "Yessir, we do. Tails

together in a circle, everybody watching out for everybody else."

He nodded. "You'll never guess how these roosted. You see, our banties roosted in a plum thicket, instead of in the nice little shed we built for 'em. When the time came for roostin', every evening, that hen would fly up into the thicket, and her quail children would fly after her. But they still had quail instincts, you see, so they lined up beside her, head, tail, head, tail, head, tail, down the row. Many's the time Pa's took the lantern out there to show visitin' kinfolks our crazy quail roostin' in a tree."

Mrs. Bragg looked at him, her expression dubious. "You sure that's true, Sol, or did you just you make it up?"

"I swear to gracious, that's just exactly what happened. For a while it was talked about all over Cotton County. That happened right after Preacher Samuels was visitin' us after Gramma's funeral. He was out on the porch talkin' with Pa and watching the quail runnin' after their mama when the dog came dashin' by.

"Those little fellows took off like sky rockets. Their mama looked up and started runnin' in circles, callin' at the top of her voice for her babies to come back down to her right that minute.

"We all just about fell off the porch laughin'. I thought Mr. Samuels was goin' to bust his suspenders, he got so tickled. His eyes watered and his face got red, and he nearly choked.

"That night Pa took him out to see the bunch roostin' in the plum tree and he was mightily impressed. He spread the word all over the county, and we had quite a few folks come all the way down there to see. There's prob'ly some old codger still around who did that, in fact. You just ask around." He plopped the legs of his chair down and spat into his snuff can again.

"But that wasn't the end of the story. We ended up with five quail, but two of them paired off and went wild. The last one, all by itself, ran with our chickens, even after the old mama banty died. It was funny to see him duck-leggin' it after Ma's big white leghorns when they strolled across the pasture.

"He roosted in the laying nests outside the big chicken house, after the plum thicket died and was cut down. Finally he disappeared, but a couple of years later he was still alive. An old black lady who lived on the next farm told my Pa that she had a crazy quail come into her kitchen with her chickens, so we knew that little bantam-quail hadn't forgot his raising."

The little bantam in the yard cocked her head sideways and clucked. Her chicks came running to huddle around her as she stalked off to the other side of the chinaberry, where the dust lay smooth and untroubled.

Mrs. Bragg stared at Sol. "I'd swear that chicken thought you were talking about her," she said. "And she didn't appreciate it one bit."

Will Henry almost snickered, but he managed to conceal it with a gulp of strawberry pop. Tim and Les and Fane looked at each other solemnly. Then they rose and took their empty bottles to the wooden case lying against the store's wall.

Chuck, in his usual deliberate manner, finished his pop while digesting this new information. Then he replaced his own empty in the crate and jumped down off the porch.

"Shooooo!" he yelled, as he dashed around the chinaberry tree.

The hen shot up on gray-brown wings, and all her chicks flew too, though not as high as she. They all settled into the pomegranate bush at the edge of the yard and sat there making irritated sounds in their throats until the boy returned to the porch.

Will Henry, outdone for once, handed Mrs. Bragg his bottle and stalked off to his bicycle. Chuck let him get a good distance up the road. Then he turned and winked at the adults on the porch before mounting his own bike and taking out after his cousin and best friend.

Sol grinned at Mr. Bragg, who sighed deeply. "Boys!" he grunted, rising painfully to her feet. "Just boys, every last one of you."

The screen door closed behind her, making the Levi Garret Snuff sign flap against the wire netting like a round of applause.

The adjoining farm to that on which I was raised contained the remnants of that ancient car, still parked where it had hit the tree, though the shed that was built over it had long rotted away.

THE RING-TAILED SIDEWINDER

Solomon Peat hadn't a mean bone in his body. Oh, he enjoyed a good laugh at somebody else's expense, but not if he thought it would really hurt feelings or leave bad memories to fester. Even Mrs. Bragg, on whose store porch he held forth almost every day of the year, admitted that when it came to all around good nature Uncle Sol just about held the record.

The five small boys who were his most appreciative audience considered him a combination of Santa Claus and one of the good old boys in the Bible their Sunday school teacher kept telling them about. Never had they seen him truly riled. He spoke softly to everyone, and his teasing was of a gentle kind that tickled even the one being teased.

On this morning, however, he wore a frown, and even the approach of Will Henry and his cohort didn't bring his usual grin to his face. He kept glaring at the antique Studebaker car that was parked beside the store, as if the very sight of it made him angry.

The thing was a work of art, restored to a condition probably better than it had been when it was new. The polish was almost blinding. Will Henry couldn't imagine what there could be about the vehicle that would make Uncle Sol look the way he did.

He followed Chuck up the steps and stood beside their great-uncle, unconsciously sticking his thumbs into his pockets just the way Sol did. Their friend Tim and his brothers, coming up the road from their riverside farm, stopped and examined the Studebaker admiringly until Sol reached into his pocket and jingled quarters suggestively. That brought all the boys to attention at once.

The owner of the Studebaker came out of the store, and he almost distracted the five boys from their strawberry pop. He wore a long duster coat and an old-fashioned hat. He carried a walking cane with a brass handle and tip.

"You been to one of them antique car rallies," Will Henry said in a longing tone. "I always wanted to see all the different kinds and the costumes and such."

The fellow chuckled. "You haven't lived till you get together with all us nuts who love the old cars. One day maybe you can get to one. But right now I'm late and I have to get to Tompkins before ten o'clock. Took a wrong turn back along the state highway and wound up here—didn't even know where here was, till the lady inside told me. You take care, you hear?" He jumped off the edge of the porch, spry as somebody half his age, and soon the old car was chugging away up the dusty road.

The boys went inside after their pop and returned to find Sol sitting in his chair, still glowering. Will Henry couldn't stand it a minute longer. "Uncle Sol," he said, "I never saw you like this before. You mad at us?"

The old man's faded blue-denim eyes widened. "I'm sorry, boys. It's just the sight of that...that...." He glanced guiltily at the screen door, behind which Mrs. Bragg was almost certainly lurking and took a deep breath. "That gol-darned car set me off, and I'd never have thought that could happen again. Something about that model of Studebaker just makes me boil."

"You have a wreck in one?" Chuck asked, licking his strawberry coated lips. "Dad never liked Fords again after that wreck he had in Templeton, back a ways."

Sol shook his head, sending his scanty white hair flopping over his ear. "No, it's not that. It's just—well, I guess I'd better tell you about Mama's Uncle Spencer. Meanest man ever wore boot leather. His family was scared to death of him, and his neighbors hated to see him comin' down the road." Sol took out his snuff can and carefully spat tobacco juice into it, put the top back on, and returned the can to his pocket.

"I never met him, you understand, but Ma went over to his farm, back when I was little, to nurse his wife when she had their tenth baby. Nobody else would do it, you understand, and Ma was too soft-hearted to let the poor woman do without somebody to take care of things. She knowed Spencer would let things go to pot before he'd lift a hand to help her or to take care of his other young'uns. As for hirin' somebody to come and help—the old reprobate would've died before he spent a dime on his family. Had money buried all over the place in canning jars, Ma said."

Letitia Bragg stumped out onto the porch and sank into

her sagging rocker. "How did she know about that? I wouldn't think that kind of man would tell anybody where he kept his cash." She fanned herself with her handkerchief as she settled back to enjoy the story.

"Ma saw him dig up a bunch of 'em when he bought his brand...new...Studebaker," Sol said. "In fact, he got her to help him hold the sack he poured the money out into.... Gold, he had, which was still legal tender, way back then. And not dollar gold pieces, either. Most of 'em was fifty-dollar coins, she told me.

"He got ready and hitched up his mare to his buggy and set off for town. Never told his wife anything about what he intended to do, either. Ma cleaned and cooked and helped Aunt Lissie tend to the baby, and the day passed by. About four o'clock in the afternoon Ma heard something comin' up the lane to the house, chuggin' and bumpin' and blarin' like a bull calf from time to time.

"Into the yard come a car with the salesman drivin' and Uncle Spencer sittin' beside him, holdin' on like grim death. Another car was followin' them; both pulled up beside the wood shed, and the men got out.

"Ma was always curious as a cat, so she managed to make some trips out after wood while they was palaverin'. Seems the salesman wanted Spencer to let him teach him how to drive his new car, but Spencer, bein' who he was, felt like he knew everythin' there was to know in all the world and didn't want to bother with that. So after a while the men left in the other car."

"What did they do with the mare and the buggy?" Will Henry asked.

"Oh, Spencer's wife had a nephew lived in town, and they left the rig with him. But it was what Spencer did after he got home that still makes me mad."

"And what was that?" Mrs. Bragg asked. "Seems as if somethin' that happened when you were a little boy wouldn't still have the power to make you mad after sixty or seventy years."

"I'm not done with the story," Sol grunted. "You just listen." He shifted his weight and stared off across the pine trees beyond the road.

"Ma said Spencer waited till the other car was all the way out of earshot before he got in the new one and called her out to turn the crank. Those old timey cars were hard to crank, I tell you, and he had no business askin' Ma to do that for him, but she did. Took a while before he caught on how to advance the spark so's the motor would catch up, but finally he did. Ma stepped back and laid the crank, which was a sort of bent metal handle that fitted into the front of the motor, down beside the pomegranate bush.

"By that time the entire family, except for Lissie and the new baby, was out on the back porch, just about out of their heads with excitement. Not one of those children ever dreamed their daddy would buy an automobile. They waited for him to show off his drivin', and by golly that's just what he did.

"Once he figured out how to shift, he jammed it into gear and poured on the gas. That car shot backward into the big old hickory tree beside the house and just about shook the old man's teeth out of his head.

"Anybody but Spencer would've felt sheepish and tried again. Not that crazy old b...basket. He jumped out and ran past the woodpile, picking up a stick of stovewood as he came after Ma. 'You fool woman, now look what you made me do?' he kept yellin' at her. He hit her a couple of good licks before she realized what was happenin'. Knocked out some teeth over at the side and near broke her left arm when she flung it up to protect herself."

"My Lord, Sol! What did she do?" Mrs. Bragg asked, leaning forward. "I'd have just about killed any man who did that to me."

"Ma didn't just stand there and take it like Lissie had always done. She grabbed that crank out from under the bush and laid into the old man. Broke his collarbone, cost him more teeth than he cost her, and laid his scalp open till he looked like he'd been scalped by Injuns. Before she was done, he was runnin' around and around the yard like a chicken that's about to get the axe, with her whalin' away at him every chance she got.

"The young'uns was yellin' and cryin' and shoutin' till poor Lissie come creepin' out to see what it was all about. Nearly shocked her out of her wits when she saw somebody standin' up to Spencer and gettin' the best of him. A while later, Ma whittled her a good solid knobstick and showed her how to use it. Spencer acted a lot better to her and the children after that."

"What happened to the car?" Chuck inquired. "A brand new car like that shouldn't be hurt too bad just by backing into a tree."

Sol's frown eased. "That was the funniest thing of all," he said. "The old man paid seven hundred dollars for that car, but after that he left it right where it was and built a shed over it. Never moved it a peg from that spot for the rest of his life. Far as I know, it's still there, or what's left of it, out in the woods that took over the farm after Spencer died and the house burned down. Some collector like that fellow who just left would prob'ly be mighty glad to get it, too."

"What a waste," Mrs. Bragg said. "All that money just lost, and him with a family, too."

"They'd never have seen a dime of it," Sol assured her. "Any money there was, Spencer kept it and used it for his own purposes, even though everybody in the family, down to the littlest ones, worked from can to can't to make a livin'. That's the way it used to be in the old redneck fam'lies down here in the bottomlands." He folded his hands over his belly and looked solemn.

"I heard a man say, once, that he didn't believe in women workin'. I happened to know that he was raising broiler chickens, which is one of the worst jobs ever invented, and his wife did most of the work. I couldn't keep my mouth shut, so I asked him, 'Bill, doesn't your wife work in your chicken houses?'

"He looked startled for a minute. Then he said, 'Oh, that's all right. She don't get PAID for it.'"

Mrs Bragg's chair gave an anguished shriek as she sprang (somewhat clumsily) to her feet. "Solomon Peat, he actually SAID that? I knew there were a lot of Neanderthals living around here, but that does beat them all." She slammed the screen behind her as she took refuge inside the store.

"What happened after your mama finished beating up her uncle?" Tim asked, sounding a bit timid. Inquiring into the doings of white people was something his family seldom did.

"Well, Ma stayed there till Lissie was on her feet again, and she left her in better shape than she found her, too. Once that woman learned that hitting hurt Spencer as much as it did her, she never forgot it. Ma told me, once I was bigger, that her uncle never even tried to hit his wife, after the first time she whaled him with that knobstick.

"But he didn't exactly reform, either. Once Ma was out of the house, Spencer went out and bought a couple of gallons of white lightnin'. Took it home and got into bed and drank it all up in just a couple of days. Lissie told Ma he had the shotgun in there and threatened to shoot anybody who came in the door, but she didn't care. She didn't want to see him, anyway.

"He stayed there for a week, stinkin' drunk, and not once did she offer to feed him or to change his bedding or anything. When he came out at last he was a mighty sick puppy, I suspect. The fact that nobody cared whether he was mad and drunk or not seems to have broke his spirit.

"But Ma never forgave him for hittin' her with that stick of stovewood. She never had a thing more to do with him, though she kept in touch with Lissie and the young'uns. Every time I saw her take out her bridge with the three false teeth in it, I got mad all over again at that ring-tailed sidewinder who'd do such a fool stunt and try to punish somebody who was trying to help him out."

He sighed, and inside the store Mrs. Bragg sighed, too. "Can't say I really blame you," she said. "I'll remember him the next time I see one of those antique cars." There was a pause. Then she asked, "You reckon you could find that old car, out there in the woods?"

Sol grinned, and Will Henry choked on his pop. If there was the slightest chance of making a profit, Mrs. Bragg was always right in there figuring how to do it.

My family and I milked right through a tornado, in the winter of 1949-50. It happened pretty much as described— who could improve on that?

A BIG WIND ON A DARK NIGHT

Solomon Peat had a sort of family reunion once a year. That happened when his cousin Willa, who disliked most of the other side of the family, took her annual trip to visit her son in Washington State. As soon as her coat-tail disappeared onto the bus, Sol would send out the word to his many assorted friends and shirt-tail kin to assemble at his house on the next Saturday night.

He'd get Mrs. Bragg to order batches of sandwich makings, bread and buns, cookies and pop, beer for the men to drink secretly out behind the kitchen, and pounds and pounds of wieners, which he knew his small great-nephews and nieces dearly loved. Because he felt as if the little black boys were also his kin, he always invited their entire families, and anybody who was officially kin and didn't like it could stay home and count grasshoppers.

Such a reunion was scheduled for the last Saturday in July, and he had already hired Mandy Farmer and her daughters to do the cooking and watch over the food and clean up afterward. They worked cheap for Sol, because they could eat and talk and drink as much as any guest, listen to Uncle Sol's tales, and get paid besides.

Will Henry, Chuck, Tim, Les, and Fain were allowed to sit up as late as the party lasted, which sometimes was until far into the early morning. Of course, they always went to sleep about midnight, try as hard as they might to last out the big folks. Being an entire year older, this time, they expected to make it all the way through.

That was a hot weekend, as usually happens in East Texas in July. The sky was like a griddle, and even the pine trees looked wilted, but by the time everybody arrived, the sun was setting and a line of clouds had covered the northwest. That eased off the heat a bit, and games of horseshoes and jacks and marbles sprang up in likely spots on the lawn.

Sol was pottering around, going from the kitchen to the front porch and back as he oversaw the distribution of food and drink to his far-flung clan. They ate outside, because Sol didn't believe in air conditioning, and it was cooler on the grass under the huge magnolia and oak trees. Mandy and Leela tracked back and forth with pitchers of lemonade and iced tea, their mahogany faces damp with sweat from the boiling wieners in the kitchen, where Nancy made hot dogs as fast as her hands could work.

By the time everybody was fed too full to pursue any game, darkness had fallen and the night was studded with fireflies and intermittent flashes of lightning in the distance. That was when Sol called them all into his huge combined parlor and sitting room, with the double doors open wide between, and gestured for them to sit down.

They did that more quickly than anyone might have

guessed, for they knew that Solomon was going to tell stories. Every one of his guests, black or white, old or young, had grown up on a steady diet of those, and nobody ever lost his or her taste for them.

As the last restless youngster settled onto the polished pine floor, the lights flickered and a long rush of wind bent the trees outside, sending a cool gust through the house. Sol sighed and leaned back in his rocker. "Feels mighty good," he said. "There's nothing like a thunderstorm to cool things off. Reminds me of another night, twenty years back."

A crash of thunder interrupted him, and the wind came again, making the old house creak and pop as loose twigs battered against it. Sol nodded. "Sounds a lot like that January night, all right. It got dark as Egypt, just like it's doing now."

A battery of distant lightning and thunder interrupted him again, and a scatter of raindrops drummed on the roof. Will Henry and Chuck, who were sitting close to the old man's knees, scooted up even closer.

"What happened, Uncle Sol?" Will Henry asked. "Where were you?"

"I was helpin' out my Cousin Betty. She and her husband and their little boy ran a good-sized dairy farm outside Templeton, all by themselves. Bradley, her man, got bad sick, and the work they had to do couldn't be done by one person, no way, no how. I was retired from the mill by then, and my wife Sarah Vee told me I ought to go out and help, since nobody else in the connection seemed willing to.

"She was a mighty persuasive lady, and I knew if I was to rest easy at home I'd better do like she suggested.

So I taken off in the pickup and lent a hand.

"January's not a real good month to work on a dairy. Your hands stay cold, and your feet stay damp, and the cow-lots are deep in mud. That had been a fairly warm month, though, so I thought I'd lucked out, at least for a while.

"We went along milkin' and hayin' and milkin' again for three days. They had their cows trained so well—used one of them old McCormick-Deering double unit milkers that did two cows at once, and every pair of cows knew their turn and where to go in the barn.

"It was kind of like workin' a bunch of circus ponies. They'd trot right in and stick their heads into the stalls to be hooked up. Not many of them were kickers, either.

"There was even one cow that got to needin' to pee real bad every time she let her milk down. She'd start dancin' around with her hind feet, and Betty would take off the milker, turn loose her head-stall, and let her go outside. She'd do her thing and come back in, and we'd go right on again. It was a fair treat, even with all the work, 'cause they had their business all organized and easy to take care of."

Letitia Bragg, sociable for once, was sitting in a deep chair across the room, and now she looked up at Sol, her eyes keen and skeptical. "Solomon, I never heard of house-breaking a cow. You sure this is the truth?"

Sol sighed. "I just dunno why you keep on doubtin' my word, Letitia. This here is somethin' that happened so recent you can call up and ask Cousin Betty herself. I'll give you her phone number...she lives in Tompkins now, since Bradley died an' she sold the farm."

Mrs. Bragg nodded as if satisfied, and Sol went on,

"One evening we had started milkin' a little late because the cows seemed nervous an' twitchy an' we had a time gettin' 'em to come out of the pasture. We turned on the big light out back of the dairy barn and started in, and the lightnin' and thunder came rolling across the big hills to the southwest, soundin' like a buffalo stampede.

"We shut the big doors an' the windows and kept on milkin'. When it started to rain, the noise on the tin roof was so loud you couldn't hear yourself think. I was stripping out the cows into one of those buckets with the closed top with just a little hole in it.

"First thing I knew there come a great big crash. The double doors bowed inward like they was about to bust, and the room filled up with sweetgum balls and leaves. Even got into that bucket, that you could hardly put your fist into. And that barn was closed up tight, too. How they got in I couldn't figure.

"Now you got to recall that back then if a little old cloud the size of your hat would come up, they'd lose their electricity, out there where Betty lived. The lights never blinked. The milkers went right on chuggin', and when we opened the doors to let in the next pair of cows they ran in like the devil his own self was behind 'em.

"Betty stared out toward the back lot behind the dairy barn, and I saw her stiffen. 'Sol,' she said, 'the calf shed's gone. Old Mary's new calf was in it. I think that was a tornado, Sol.' She sounded pretty shaken up, so I got the milkers all settled and went to see, too. Sure enough, there was no sign of the stout shed where she put baby calves while she was weanin' 'em.

"I looked over at the big hay barn, and there came Betty's son Ted, drippin' wet, sloshing through the mud.

'Mama,' he yelled, 'part of the barn roof's been blown away, and our hay's gettin' wet!'

"I knew how hard they'd all worked that summer, baling that hay, and I turned and said, 'You take care here, and I'll go help Teddy move the hay. Can't risk losin' your winter feed.'"

"You mean that was a tornado that went over you while you were milking?" Chuck asked. "And you never knew it till later?"

"Right." Uncle Sol rocked gently, rocking himself with one toe. "We were almost through milking when Ted came over, and by the time he and I moved about fifty bales of hay back under the remaining roof, Betty had finished milking and had the equipment and the barn clean, too. Time we got to the house it was later than usual, and Bradley had gotten out of bed to peep out and see if we were on our way.

"'I thought I heard a freight train,' he said when we got inside. 'The wind has been something fierce. Everything go all right?'

"Betty looked at me, and I started to laugh, and little Ted joined in. Bradley looked as if he thought the whole kit and biling of us had gone crazy before we calmed down enough to tell him what had happened.

"Turned out, that tornado came right at us over the hills, ripped across the cow lot, carried away the calf shed and moved the calf over one lot and down two. The little fellow was stove up for a few days, but nothing was broke.

"Besides carryin' away the shed, it took off about a quarter of the barn roof, neat as if it had used shears, and tore Betty's pig shelter to flinders. Then it made a track through the woods to the northeast and headed for the little town a few miles off. Left a trail of downed trees like a crazy lumberjack.

"The next day we just took off, after we got through in the barn, and followed that track. Bundled up Bradley and took him, too. The storm went across the highway and tore up the Christian Church for the third time. Busted the post office all to pieces and left the rest of the little old brick buildings too flimsy to use.

"After it left there, it kept right on, still on the ground. Up the road a way, it had veered back to the west, and went up a dirt road through thick pine woods. The pines was all wound up and wrapped around with strips of roofing tin as if they was Christmas trees. We passed where a house had been, but there was nothing left to speak of.

"Around a bend we found a floor, clean as if it had been swept, with steps on both sides of it. Right in the middle of the floor stood a green glass coal-oil lamp, sittin' there as untouched as if nothing had happened at all. Everything else was gone."

"I remember that storm," Mrs. Bragg said. She sounded even more solemn than usual. "Killed Patsy Ramsey's husband and son when it took their house off. There were folks out that way who were left with nothing but their night clothes, and a few didn't even have them left. I remember going out there with donations, days after the storm, and it looked as if the Wrath of God had struck."

Solomon nodded. "We thought so, too. It shook us all up considerably, but somethin' about the shock seemed to chirk Bradley up enough so he could get up. Before long he was back at work and I went home.

"When I told my wife what happened, she looked kind of funny. That was one strange woman, too. She started to laugh. 'Solomon Peat,' she said, 'for once you met a bigger wind than you are.'"

Will Henry and Chuck began to laugh. They curled up on the floor, holding their stomachs, and one by one the rest of the bunch began to guffaw. Mrs. Bragg's deep chuckle joined the chorus.

A jolt of wind hit the house, and the lights went out. That didn't leave them in darkness, however, for the lightning outside was almost as steady and bright as the electrics had been. There came a distant roar, and everyone hit the floor.

It passed in the distance, and Sol said, "It missed us, this time." He scratched a match and lit the candle always kept in the library table drawer against a failure of electricity. The warm light wasn't enough to fill the room, but it allowed the assembled kinfolk and friends to get themselves and their families together.

It was time to go home, for the rain had become a steady roar that promised to last all night. Will Henry joined his parents and turned to look back from the front door.

Mrs. Bragg was standing beside Sol's rocker, looking down at him. "Solomon Peat," she said, "It's not every storyteller who can conjure up a storm, just to illustrate his tales. I've got to hand it to you—this was the best reunion you ever threw, and you've done some humdingers."

Will Henry grinned in the darkness as he followed his father in a dash for the car. He agreed completely. A party at Uncle Sol's was unpredictable, at any time, and this one was by far the best of all.

My mother was alive with magic at Christmas time. She made everything glitter with her own variety of fairy dust, and she made the most attractive cloth dolls you could ever dream of.

CHRISTMAS WAS THE NEATEST TIME

Sleet was pattering against the tin roof of Mrs. Bragg's store. The frozen grass crunched underfoot as Will Henry trudged along toward the steps, which turned out to be slippery as glass. Cold as it was, Mrs. Bragg's holly wreath on the screen door cheered him up as he crossed the porch.

It was too early for many to have made it in to Possum Creek. The schools were closed, many of the roads being impassable, for an ice storm had preceded the sleet. The pine forest looked as if it had been decorated by a lavish hand, and even the gloomy light through the clouds made the trees and weeds sparkle.

Feeling as if his nose was about to drop off, the boy opened the door and stepped into the warmth of the store, where the wood stove, stuffed with pine knots, was sending out a blast of heat. Uncle Solomon Peat, driven from his customary perch on the porch, was sitting on a stool behind the heater, his back against the wall.

Above his head an old-fashioned crepe paper bell, the kind that folded flat but unfolded into a three-dimensional honeycomb, swung in the draft from the doorway. Shiny strips of red and silver foil were draped along the counter and the top shelves, making the dim little store seem festive.

Will Henry sighed as he pulled off his heavy coat and took off the wool scarf his mother had wrapped around his head, over his most earnest protests. "The little kids at home got so rambunctious I just had to get out of the house. Mama finally said I could come. I'm sure glad you came, too, Uncle Sol. I thought it might be too cold for you to get out," he said to his great-uncle.

He hung his wraps carefully on Mrs. Bragg's antique hat-stand and sat on a barrel beside Sol, out of the way of any customers who might venture out.

Sol grunted. "It'll be a bad day, sure enough, when I stay home while Willa's in a housecleaning mood. That woman gets fixey at the oddest times—why clean house when it's so cold anybody in her sane senses ought to sit down, read a book, and drink hot chocolate?

Mrs. Bragg, for once, said nothing about people who weren't customers hanging around the store. If Will Henry hadn't felt the thought to be disrespectful, he would have said she was lonely, too, at the thought of spending a day in the store with nobody there to fuss at.

This time she surprised the socks off him. "Speaking of hot chocolate," she said, "I've got a kettle of hot water sitting right there on that heater. Let's open a box of instant cocoa and have us a cup."

Sol's eyes went so wide there was a strip of white all

the way around the faded blue of his eyes. "That's mighty thoughtful of you, Letitia," he said. "You want me to get the mugs down?"

There was a line of cup hooks high on the wall behind the counter, each holding a mug with a name printed on it in Magic Marker.

Will Henry jumped up. "Let me do it, Mrs. Bragg. I'll hand 'em down to you."

Soon the three were sitting beside the stove, soaking in heat, inside and outside. A strip of shiny stuff slid down and tickled Sol's ear, and he rose to hook it back up. "Makes me think of Ma, this time of year," he said, looking wistful.

"I still hear some of the old folks say your mama was a great hand for Christmas," Mrs. Bragg said. "Some still talk about her cookies and her fruitcake and her decorations. Hard to see how she came up with all her fixings, back when folks had no money to speak of."

"Didn't take money for Ma to make things cheerful," Sol said. "She would take the silver paper other people threw away and wrap it around sweetgum balls. Made the prettiest decorations you ever saw. She painted some of 'em with gold paint, too.

"Pine cones were almost her favorites, though. She'd saw them in half and glue 'em to boards cut in circles. The cones looked like flowers, let me tell you. Then she'd paint 'em red and gold, stick holly everywhere there was space for it, and she had a wreath that looked like a million dollars."

"How many children did she have to fix for?" Mrs. Bragg asked. "I know about your brother Yale and your younger brother William, Will Henry's and Chuck's granddaddy, but I thought you had some sisters, too."

"Oh, we did. Just didn't pay much mind to 'em, since they was years and years younger than William. Three sisters, we had, Janey, Lucy, and Dovie. So that made six of us Ma could scheme and work and finagle to have presents for on Christmas."

"But if there wasn't any money, how did she buy presents?" asked Will Henry, ever practical. "Every year Papa says Mama is going to bankrupt him if she keeps ordering stuff and makin' trips to town."

"Why," said Sol, "she didn't need money. She made just about everything herself. When we were little, she'd cut up old velvet or plush jackets and skirts or wool shirts and flannel nightgowns and make stuffed animals that were the cutest things you ever saw. I've still got the black velvet kitten I got when I was about four years old. Its nap is pretty worn down, and the button eyes came off a long time ago, but it's still in a box where my wife put it away, forty years ago.

"Why, one year Ma made twenty-two stuffed animals for us and the nephews and nieces—cats and dogs and ponies and such. She whittled a jointed figure, too, with a hole in its back for a dowel, painted it up bright, and Yale got that. He'd put a thin piece of board under him, sit straddle of it, and beat on it, and that little man would dance on the other end. I bet his kids still have that thing, and I'd wager it still dances, if anybody thinks to get it out and try."

Will Henry finished his mug of cocoa and set it on the shelf behind the counter. "But what about presents for the grown folks? They don't like toys and such. How did she manage that?"

"She'd make Pa new shirts for Christmas, or hem him a set of handkerchiefs or knit him warm socks to wear when he went out in the cold to feed the livestock. It's only little 'uns that don't like to get clothes for presents," Sol told him. "She was always workin' on a quilt for somebody in the connection, too, and when she set down in the evenin', she would crochet doilies and lace collars and such that looked like snowflakes. Never spent an idle moment in her life, did Ma."

He got that faraway look that told his listeners he was seeing the past again. "We had the best time of anybody. I knew a lot of folks whose parents were so harsh and stern with 'em the kids never drew an easy breath. My folks weren't like that.

"Don't think we didn't get it good and proper when we did somethin' wrong, now, but most of the time we got along fine. Pa was the world's best storyteller, and while we worked in the fields he'd keep us laughin' like crazy.

"When we sat down to Ma's table, she'd have it fixed nice, with the best smellin' food you ever laid a nose to. At Christmas time, you could mighty near float on the good smells comin' out of her kitchen. She'd have all kinds of candies and cookies, made with honey and molasses and flour and hickory nuts and pecans.

"But the best time was when her eyes would start to sparkle and she'd say, 'It's time to go get the greenery.' That meant the tree and bamboo vines and mistletoe to decorate the house. Pa'd roll out the wagon and hitch up the mule. We'd pile into the back, first three of us, then later on six of us, with the little girls, and we'd go bumpin' into the woods and over into the thicket where the young pines grew.

"We'd sing 'Jingle Bells' or 'Silent Night' or 'Joy to the World' fit to scare the crows and hawks, too. It was the best kind of time there was, all of us together, singin'. We'd get the tree first, and that would take quite a while. First Pa would find one, but Ma would locate a thin patch on it. Then Yale would find a better one. Sometimes it took a whole mornin' just to decide which was the best.

"Then Pa'd get the axe out of the wagon and trim off the lowest branches to get to the trunk. With two or three whacks, he'd have it down, for Pa was an axeman to beat all. We'd grab the tree by the raw end and pull it so we didn't mess up the branches, load it in the wagon, and go back into the woods for the other greenery.

"There was a big holly tree that was Ma's pet. We trimmed it for years without ever messin' up its shape or leavin' it bare-lookin'. Then Pa would drive over to the oak that had the best mistletoe in the county, 'way up high in its top. He'd take the .22 rifle and shoot off a bunch, neat as a pin, for he'd hit it right where the stem came out of the tree. He was a mighty good shot, too, my Pa."

Will Henry was wiggling on his seat, envisioning everything. "What a neat way to get your stuff!"

"After the mistletoe, we'd move along to the creek, where rattan and honeysuckle and bamboo vines grew all over the bushes and up the trees. Ma'd pick out a tall tree with long trailers of bamboo vine running up it, and Yale and me'd grab hold and pull it down, bit by bit, till it come loose and we'd tumble in the dead leaves, laughin' fit to kill. It was the best of times, like old man Dickens said in his book." Sol sighed and wiped his eyes with his blue bandana.

"Not too many families knew how to have that much

fun together," Mrs. Bragg said, setting her feet on the apron of the heater. "My family was solemn and proper and scared to do anything different from everybody else. Every day of my life I heard somebody ask, 'What will people think?' Now I'm old enough to die, I realize most people don't think much, and probably not at all about what I'm doing, but it's too late to break the habit.

"You were lucky, Sol, to grow up like that. Maybe that's why you get along so well with children."

Sol nodded. "You're right, Letitia. But just wait. The best part, maybe, was that night when chores was done and supper was over and cleaned up after, and we got together in the big parlor to set up the tree. Everybody had his own job, you have to understand.

"The ones too little to be trusted up high put on the decorations down low, and Ma never told 'em she went back after bedtime and moved ornaments around to fill up bare spots. Pa did the top, bein' tallest of us all, and the angel he fixed up there was really pretty. Ma had made it out of a tin can and gold paint and sequins off somethin' her sister gave her. It was just handsome!

"Yale put on the icicles, which was more of that silver paper, cut in real thin strips, and William fixed up the bird nests."

"Bird nests?" Will Henry sat up straight and stared. "What kind of bird nests?"

"The ones Ma made out of that gray fungus that grows on dead stumps. She'd paint 'em gold or silver and glue the bits together till a real bird would've been proud to own 'em. Then she'd dye acorns all sorts of colors, all dark, of course, because the acorns were dark, but once William put 'em into the nests the effect was mighty colorful."

"What did you do, Sol?" Mrs. Bragg asked. "You've never yet said."

Uncle Sol blushed. Actually blushed, red as a rose. "Well, Letitia, You've got to understand that once I passed about nine years old, I was the clumsiest boy you ever did see or hear of. I could walk across the floor and fall three times. I could knock over things ten feet away, and anything breakable wasn't safe if I was in the room.

"That was why Pa made me the official Christmas storyteller. He'd set me safely in the corner by the stove and hand me the Bible or one of his books that had belonged to his own Pa, and tell me to read aloud while they worked. I did that for a while. Then I started makin' up stories of my own, 'cause we all knew the old ones, word for word. I guess that's why I still love to tell stories, if truth be known."

"Then what would you do?" Will Henry asked. "After fixin' up the tree."

"Oh, we'd light the candles. VERY careful they had to be with that. There was little tin holders shaped like flowers and held with clips, and every one held a tiny little candle. When they was all lit, it was mighty nice to look at, but they never let me get near the tree when the candles was burnin'. Wasn't safe, you understand. I could've burned down the whole entire place.

"Then we'd sit around on the parlor settee and the nice chairs—never used 'em otherwise—and just look at that tree and say to each other, "This is the prettiest one ever.""

His blue eyes were bright with tears. "And every year that was just exactly the truth, too."

A gust of sleet spattered against the tin roof. Will

Henry shivered deliciously, sitting there in the warm, his stomach filled with hot cocoa, his mind full of bright images.

But Uncle Sol was silent, still reliving the childhood that was still so much a part of him.

Naming no names, this family lived as neighbors to mine when we lived in town. The boy in the chicken house may still be alive!

NIGHT OWL

It had been a long two weeks for Solomon Peat. Will Henry and Chuck had spent the first two weeks of summer vacation in Templeton with Will Henry's Aunt Elissa and her sons, leaving no regular listeners on Mrs. Bragg's porch. The occasional customers seldom had time to listen to an entire story, and Mrs. Bragg always tried to seem too busy with her store to pay attention, though he knew she did.

Even Tim and Les and Fane had been kept busy in their mother's garden, picking beans and shelling peas and helping with canning tomatoes. When their mother put up food for the winter, she did an all-out job of it.

Today was Saturday, however, and as the old fellow stumped up onto the porch and took his place in the hickory splint chair against the wall, he could see two small shapes whirling up the road, trailed by wisps of dust kicked up by their bicycle wheels. As Tim's mother went to town on Saturdays, all three of the small black boys were already there, waiting for him.

Sol began to grin as Will Henry and Chuck pulled up with a flourish and propped their bikes against the chinaberry tree. Looking self consciously nonchalant, they climbed the steps and reached into their pockets.

"Today's our treat," Will Henry told Sol. "Aunt Lissa gave me 'n' Chuck five dollars apiece. You all want the regular?"

Sol nodded, and Tim and his brothers nodded, too. In a moment everyone on the porch was occupied with a frosty bottle of strawberry pop. Six sighs of satisfaction rose into the pine and dust-scented air.

With elaborate casualness, Sol asked, "So what did you two find to do for a whole two weeks in town?"

Chuck nodded at Will Henry, who took another sip and set his bottle between his skinned knee and the wall of the porch. "We went to the new movie house. Not the one downtown—they're goin' to close that one—but the brand new one in the shopping center out on the edge of town.

"Saw the best movie ever, all about Luke Skywalker and Princess Layer and aliens and bad guys. You ought to go see it, Uncle Sol. It's great."

Sol had heard more than he wanted to about that movie, but he was interested in the location of the theater. "Is that up on the north side where the big creek comes down and crosses the road? Used to be farms all out there, when I lived in Templeton, way back when I ran that mill."

"Yessir. They've built a bank and a lot of other stuff east of the creek, besides the theater and discount store and such."

Uncle Sol began to chuckle. Will Henry pricked up his

ears, for when the round bulk of his great-uncle began to quiver, it meant a good story was on its way.

In a moment Sol wiped his eyes and settled his chair on its back two legs, leaning against the wall. "Strangest folks you ever want to see used to own the farm there. Turner Daily was the man's name, and he was sort of a scientist—bred chickens that used to win prizes at shows, and folks all over the country would order breeding stock from him.

"His wife was a naturalist. Used to keep live snakes in her vases. I knew a fellow who did yard work for her. One day she asked him to come in the house and help move some furniture. There he was heaving up one end of this great big table, and he glanced around to make sure he didn't knock a tall vase off the buffet behind him. Right then a grass snake stuck its head out to see what was goin' on.

"Almost wet himself, he told me. Bill hated snakes worse'n anybody I ever saw. He never went in that house again."

"Well, that's odd, but I don't see anything so funny about it," Chuck said around the top of his pop bottle.

"Oh, that wasn't the story. It's just sort of what they call background. Their son was the weird one. There was tales all over the school about some of the things he'd do. Nothing wicked, just strange as all get-out. His daddy used to get mad about it, but his mama paid no attention. She was sort of proud of being an oddball."

"You talkin' about Lillian Daily?" Mrs. Bragg's gruff voice asked from inside the store. "Craziest woman ever to wear shoe-leather. Cleaned her house on Sundays. Spent the rest of the week out in the woods catchin' critters."

Uncle Sol raised his voice a bit, knowing he'd snared her. That was his underlying aim, when he told a tale. If he could get Mrs. Bragg to listening, it made his day.

"Yes, ma'am. That boy of hers—what was his name, now?"

"Lucius. Heathen name, it always sounded to me, and I wouldn't be surprised if that was what sent him off the rails, there at the end." Mrs. Bragg snorted. "He up and went to Africa, of all things, and got killed in some kind of war over there."

"Thank you, my dear," Sol said. "Lucius was so quiet his daddy paid no attention to him and never thought about him unless he was right under foot. Anyway, somethin' had been botherin' Turner's chickens in the night. He'd go out in the morning and his breeding hens would be fussin', and the egg count went down considerable.

"He hatched the eggs in an incubator, you see, and sold chicks for big money, at least for them days. It meant a good part of his income. So naturally he was upset. He determined he was goin' to set up at night until he found what was gettin' into the henhouse.

"Bein' Turner, he said nothing to anybody, just laid awake till about midnight with his ears peeled for any unusual ruckus in the back pen. He was about to go to sleep, finally, when he heard a squawk.

"He got up and dressed. Got a powerful flashlight and a baseball bat and snuck out through the back garden in his bedroom slippers. He climbed the gate so it wouldn't squeak and cracked open the henhouse door."

Sol glanced around at the line of intent faces, mouths rimmed with red from forgotten soda-pop. He had them in his hand now, he knew. A creak from inside the store told him Mrs. Bragg had shifted her weight forward in her worn rocker, waiting for the climax.

"He listened for a minute and he could hear the hens sort of moving and grumbling like they do in the night, so he knew something was in there with 'em. He clicked on the flashlight and shined it toward the laying nests, but there wasn't anything unusual there.

"He had built long roosts, sort of like pole steps, that slanted from the floor to the angle where the roof hit the wall, and he ran the light along every pole, beginning at the bottom. Nothing there.

"He scanned the next pole, but he couldn't see a thing. The third was the same, but when the light hit the fourth layer, he almost lost it. A big black shape was there, and two shiny-bright eyes was starin' at him out of a dark face.

"If it was an owl, it was the godawfullest biggest one he'd ever heard of. It just set there, starin' at him, never movin' or makin' a sound."

Now the boys had leaned forward, eyes wide, holding their breath. Sol paused for a long moment to get his effect.

"Turner raised that bat and let the thing have it right in the head, whack. It dropped to the floor and flopped around, and he caught it and dragged it out so he'd have room to see what sort of varmint he'd knocked off the perch.

"When he turned on the flash again, out in the open, he could see better, and he almost died. It was that darn Lucius, wearin' one of them aviator caps with goggles, like young ones used to wear way back then. He had on a raincoat and that helmet, and he was sittin' on a chicken roost at midnight."

Mrs. Bragg appeared in the doorway, her own eyes wide. "Solomon Peat, do you mean that really happened? You swear it?"

"Letitia, I got the whole entire tale direct from Turner's next door neighbor, Jody Williams, who lived not a half mile from the Daily house. He saw the light and went over to see was somethin' wrong.

"There stood Turner, holdin' the boy and trying to wake him up. Williams just scooped 'em both into his pickup and headed for the hospital.

"Turner told him the whole thing from beginning to end while they rode along. Probably he never would have let it out, if he hadn't been in what you might call a state of shock."

Sol settled his round body more comfortably in his chair and looked at the row of boys. He spat neatly into the can that held his snuff-spit and grinned.

Will Henry took a long sip of pop. "I'd say that boy had some real problems," he said. "Did it hurt him bad?"

"Didn't even knock him all the way out—just addled him for a bit. He was fine the next morning and went to school—didn't act any nuttier than normal, was what I heard."

The boys looked at each other, then at Sol. Will Henry spoke for them all when he said, "You know, that isn't such a crazy thing to do. I've slid out...."—then he caught himself and tried to pretend he hadn't said a thing.

"You all stay off chicken roosts in the middle of the night," came the pronouncement from inside the store. "Get yourselves killed and what'll I do for customers?"

Which Uncle Sol knew was as close as Mrs. Bragg could possibly come to expressing her affection for the five small boys who haunted the porch of her store and swigged strawberry pop. He grunted.

"Actually," he mused, "I've been known to do crazy things from time to time in my own youth. Maybe poor old Lucius wasn't as nutty as we all thought he was. But his daddy never got over that. Quit raisin' chickens and turned to pure-bred bulls. Sold 'em to the college farm, too." He chuckled.

"I guess he figured even Lucius wouldn't ever consider goin' out at midnight to share the pen with a bunch of young bulls."

Five young heads nodded solemnly. The boys might have been tempted to see what a chicken roost was like in the middle of the night, but every one of them knew that a bull was a bull. Nobody wanted a closer acquaintance with those than was absolutely necessary.

I wish you could have heard my Dad tell this—he was with Bill in the cornfield, watching as it happened, and he still would dissolve with laughter at the memory when re-telling the tale.

SUGAR CANE

Rabbit Lucas had brought in a bunch of sugar cane from his canefield down near the river. The long bundle of purple stalks leaned against the wall on the porch of Mrs. Bragg's store, tempting her customers to shell out a dollar for a stalk or ten cents for a single joint.

Solomon Peat was already sitting in his hickory splint chair, a cane-stalk across his knees, cutting off neat rounds with his big pocket knife, with a drift of long purple peelings at his feet. For once he wasn't chewing tobacco, and his snuff can for spitting in was out of sight in his overalls pocket.

An arc of chewed and discarded pulp off the end of the porch marked the range of his spitting ability. Mrs. Bragg's big brown dog had already checked and decided that was nothing any self-respecting dog would waste time trying to eat. The chickens, being brainless to begin with, hadn't quite given up on them but were getting discouraged.

When Will Henry and Chuck came into view on their bicycles, Sol grinned. He remembered being that young, when the sugary juice of the cane filled him with delight and sent him home sticky and replete.

Before the boys got their bikes leaned against the chinaberry tree, he had two dollars in quarters ready for them. When you were a child and began chewing cane, a stalk was just barely enough.

"Sugar cane!" Will Henry murmured, as he took his dollar and headed into the store. "Seems a long time since we last had any."

When the pair came back out onto the porch, Uncle Sol was looking thoughtful, which usually indicated a story somewhere in the offing. By the time the three black boys arrived and were provided with stalks of their own, Sol was leaning his chair back against the wall, his knife safely put away, and his own stalk of cane awaiting its turn. Stories always came first, on Mrs. Bragg's porch.

There was a lull in business; Mrs. Bragg came out and plunked down into the other chair, fanning herself with a folded paper bag. "Sol, it's hot enough to cook the cans right there on the shelf," she said.

"I've got a tale will make you laugh," Sol said, and all eyes turned toward him. "About sugar cane, too. About a canefield, in fact.

"There's not many left, nowadays. Old Rabbit's the only one grows cane around here, and he's only got that one little field. But thirty years ago lots of folks grew good stands of cane, and there was several syrup mills in the county. They used to mash the stalks and boil the juice down for syrup. Ribbon cane syrup was better than anything you can find in the stores, but there got to be a pest that killed all the ribbon cane, so we get a hybrid now that just hasn't got the flavor the old kind did.

"Anyway, I'd been runnin' the new lumber mill over at Tompkins till I got sick with some bug that really got me down. I was in bed two weeks, and once I got up again I was weak and trembly.

"My wife Sarah Vee knew that as long as I was in town, the folks at the mill would call me every time anythin' at all went wrong with the operation. She got my Cousin Knox to invite us out to his farm, where there was no telephone and it was too far to come and ask me for advice.

"I was glad to go, too. Felt like I'd been wrung out and hung up to dry, I tell you. Knox was my favorite cousin on my Ma's side, and he and Mary seemed right glad to have us there. Sarah Vee liked 'em, and she always enjoyed helpin' Mary with cannin' and seein' to the children.

"Once I was well enough to get up and around, I went to the field with Knox in the afternoons. Bein' old fashioned to the bones, he still worked with mules. Gave him plenty of time to think, he used to say.

"It was almost time for his cane to ripen; the patch was down the hill from his cornfield where he was workin', and he kept an eye on it. His young mule, Coaly, was determined to get in there somehow, in spite of the electricity Knox had hooked up to the fence. A kind of blue-green box hung onto a fence post, with a battery inside, and every second or two it sent a pulse of electricity through the wire along the top of the posts."

Chuck chewed slowly on a bit of cane, letting juice dribble down his chin because he was so intent on the story. "Didn't that hurt the mule?" he asked.

Sol chuckled. "It stung him, yes, but it didn't do any damage. Many's the time I watched the big black mule try to lean his head over the top wire to get the nearest stalk, but that fence would bite him good. Got so he'd just stand off in the distance and stare at the cane. Wouldn't go any closer than ten feet, for fear it would reach out and get him again."

The old man went off into a joggle of chuckles, choked, and had to catch his breath. "But the funniest thing," he gasped, "was that preacher!"

"What preacher?" Mrs. Bragg sounded dubious, for she had told Sol more than once not to be irreverent about preachers when he talked to small boys.

"Knox had a black couple on the place, workin' on shares. Bill, the husband, was in the field with us on that particular day. His wife, Annie, was a big church-goer, and it seems like every time the door opened at their house another preacher arrived to eat a meal with 'em.

"A long black car drove up in Bill's driveway, about an hour after lunch time. Now remember that his house was right near the canefield, which was planted in a post-oak flat behind it. Bill kept watchin' and Knox kept workin', while I sat in the shade and took note of everything that went on, which wasn't much up till then.

"After just long enough for the preacher, a big fellow in a black suit, to have a snack inside Bill's house, he came out the back door, pickin' his teeth. I cocked around under my shade tree to see what he was about to do, and sure enough he wandered over to the canefield fence and looked the crop over. While it wasn't all the way ripe, the stalks nearest the fence, gettin' more sun, seemed to be just right.

"I heard Bill snicker, and Knox stopped what he was doin' and looked around. Then we all watched while the preacher took hold of the top strand of fence wire and flung up his leg to step over. Tall as he was, that leg had to be somethin' like five foot up in the air. Right in the middle of his step the jolt hit him."

Will Henry sputtered with laughter, and Uncle Sol nodded. "Sure enough, there he was, his leg way up in the air, his hand on the wire, tryin' his best to let go and step back, but before he could do it the fence would hit him again. He was jerkin' like a frog leg bein' fried, but he just couldn't seem to get loose any way he tried.

"Finally he just seemed to push himself backward and fell flat on his back in the dirt in that fancy black suit.

"I thought old Bill would bust a gut he laughed so hard, 'cause he was flat on his own back, his knees pulled up to his chest, just dyin' a'laughin'. Knox was leaned over with his hands on his knees, almost cryin' he was so tickled.

"Of course, I'd seen it comin' and wasn't quite so surprised, but still it was a sight to tickle a goat. By the time the preacher got himself out of there in his big black Cadillac, we had straightened out a little bit, but every now and then, all the rest of the afternoon, somebody'd give a chuckle and set us all off again.

"But the craziest thing of all was when we got to the house and Knox and I tried to tell our wives about it. Mary looked puzzled and Sarah Vee shook her head like we was both crazy.

"That was when I decided women don't have any sense of humor at all." He wiped his eyes, for just remembering that scene had set him off.

Letitia Bragg rose from her chair. She was trying to keep a straight face, it was plain to see, but she had to escape into the store before she disgraced herself by laughing at one of Sol's disrespectful tales. Preacher or not, the mental picture everybody had was mighty funny.

Will Henry and Chuck, Tim and Les and Fane, looked at each other and giggled. Uncle Sol picked up his cane stalk and cut a round to chew.

Nobody there would ever look at sugar cane again without seeing the preacher, his leg in the air, jerking with every pulse of that electric fence. Will Henry thought that was a mighty good memory to have, too, even at second hand.

My own brother was the trapper who pulled thirty-seven skunks out from under our house, where they had found a central-heated home for the winter.

THE SKUNK WORKS

Mrs. Bragg's sad brown dog looked even sadder than usual as he slunk into the packed dirt yard of the store and flopped down in the shade of the chinaberry tree. Uncle Sol Peat, who was sitting on the porch, and five small boys, ranged along its edge, crinkled their noses.

"Smells like old Fang's caught him a skunk," Sol sighed. "Will Henry, you take a stick and run him off into the pasture. I can't even *think*, that dog smells so strong."

All five boys hopped down and chased the unhappy dog out of skunk-smelling range. Sol, watching the pursuit, saw the animal sink into a clump of huckleberry bushes at last, and the boys came panting back to the porch to be rewarded with quarters for strawberry pop.

When they emerged from the store, already wearing strawberry colored smiles, Sol had leaned his chair back against the wall. That meant a story was on its way, everyone knew.

"I recall when I was a little feller, much smaller than

you all, except for Fane there, and my Mama sent me to stay with her sister Lissie. She and her husband Forrest had built 'em a new house when the old cabin on their place finally fell in. They picked a right pretty spot, too, on top of a long rise with big trees all around, but they didn't know at the time that they was right plunk in the middle of a highway." He glanced at the boys, who took thoughtful sips of pop.

Will Henry squinched his eyes. "How could they miss something like that?" he asked. "You can see a highway a long way off, even farther than you can see this road right here."

"It wasn't a people road," Sol said. "It was a skunk road, and not 'til summer came and the skunks decided to do their travelin' did Lissie find out what had happened. We all woke up in the middle of the night, about two days after I got there, just about stretched out stiff from the stink.

The skunks found the house in their way and just walked around it, but a skunk, even in the best mood, has considerable aroma around himself. Smelled like burnt coffee mixed with somethin' a lot worse. Seems as if havin' to detour made 'em a bit unhappy, too, so when Old Red, the bird dog, went to investigate they sprayed him good and proper."

"Just like old Fang," Chuck said around the top of his pop bottle.

"Exactly. But there was nothin' to be done about the situation—you don't pick up and move a house, or at least you didn't then, though folks seem to be doin' it more, nowadays. So I spent the summer there knowin' that most every night I'd wake up with my nose full of skunk-stink.

Wasn't much fun. When I left, it was almost Fall, so Ma figured that would solve the problems, bein' as skunks don't meander so much in cold weather."

"And did it?" came Mrs. Bragg's deep-voiced question from inside the store.

Sol winked at the boys and sipped his own soda before answering. "Well, that partic'lar problem stopped when the weather got cold and nasty. But somethin' else came up. Lissie wrote to Ma most every month, and about February we got a letter from her." He began to chuckle.

"You got to understand how that house was built. There was a big old chimney stack right in the middle that served fireplaces in two of the main rooms. The house was set up on two-foot-high brick foundations with little ventilator spaces all along the sides, like they say to do to stop dry rot and termites.

"Well they kep' a big fire goin' most of the time, because that was one cold, wet winter. Turned out the skunks thought central heatin' was a mighty good idea, and they crawled through the vents an' dug in around the base of the chimney, though nobody knew it at the time. They must've sent out invitations to all their friends and relatives, too, the way it turned out.

"One night when the family was sound asleep the skunk family seems to have had a big fallin' out among themselves and kicked up a ruckus, complete with sprays and stinks. Woke everybody up, just from the smell. Lissie was just about beside herself, wonderin' how they'd manage to live through the winter till they could do somethin' about the situation."

Mrs. Bragg clumped onto the porch and dropped into her own splint chair. "That's a puzzler. Nobody in his sane senses would crawl under a house and try to catch a whole bunch of live skunks. What on earth did they do about it?"

Sol was beaming. Getting Letitia Bragg to admit she was listening to his tales was now his major goal in life.

"You got to remember that Lissie and Forrest had a teenage boy. I was named for him, actually. Sol was about fourteen at the time and a trapper to beat all. He made his school clothes money sellin' skins of mink and squirrel tails and such to the dealers who used to buy furs around here.

"Young Sol got out his trappin' book, for he was a real believer in learnin' how to do what he wanted to before he started out. Trappin' skunks had a whole chapter to itself, too.

"There was a bamboo thicket on their farm, and they used to cut their fishin' poles there. Forrest had a whole bunch of 'em dryin' out on the rafters in the hay barn. Sol got the longest, strongest one there and wired one of his steel traps to the little end. Then he opened up the scuttle hole that let him or his daddy crawl under the house if anything needed fixin'. Left it open about a week before he set the trap.

The critters used it, too. Why go through a skinny old vent if there's a nice wide hole to use? They started goin' in and out that way, which was just what Sol wanted 'em to do. Once they was used to it and thought nothin' about it, he set his trap right there in the middle of the openin'.

"First mornin', he had a big old skunk in the trap, mad as a wet wasp. Sol grabbed the big end of the pole and started leadin' the critter away from the house, down to the stock pond.

"Now you got to remember that our breed of skunk's

got to have his back to you before he can ready, aim, fire! Long as Sol was leadin' him forwards, he couldn't do a thing to protect himself.

"They got to the pond, Lissie said, and Sol pivoted around, makin' the skunk follow the pole, and drowned him in the pond so he couldn't come back to the house, and he couldn't stink up anybody, either. Worked just like that book said it would, and Sol was mighty proud.

"Every night he set that trap, and every mornin' for thirty-seven days he led off a skunk to meet his Maker. Sold the skins for a goodly sum, too."

"Thirty-seven skunks! You've got to be exaggerating, Solomon," Mrs. Bragg objected. "How could so many get entrenched so fast?"

"Nobody ever figured that out, but someplace in the papers in Ma's trunk I've still got the letters Lissie sent. Ma never throwed anything away, and when we moved into the new house I built for my wife, Sarah Vee went through everythin'. She thought the letters and papers might be interestin' to our children. We never had any, though, so they've just set there ever since.

"An' what they *said* was thirty-seven skunks was ketched out from under Lissie's house. You better believe that they put up baby-chicken wire over the vents and they kep' that crawl hole covered from then on out. Never had no more skunks get under the house, though it was several years before the critters stopped comin' through their yard.

"They had to get a great big mean dog to do that, too. He was half German shepherd and half red wolf, a real pussy-cat to people, but he wouldn't let anythin' but the yard cats circulate inside the fence. Even birds that flew over his space got barked at good and proper.

THE LOQUAT EYES, BY ARDATH MAYHAR * 81

"He was a funny dog, too. Most of 'em, when they get sprayed by a skunk or have a good roll in some kind of dead animal, want to come right up and rub against you and lay on the porch and be chummy.

"Not old Gabriel. He'd have himself an accident, like Fang did, and he'd take off into the woods till he felt like he was respectable again. Then he'd come home and pretend nothin' at all ever happened to him."

"I wish Fang would do the same," Mrs. Bragg muttered. "Sometimes he stinks up the whole store, when he's had one of those accidents. Last month, you remember, Sol, somebody caught a big old gar down on the river and left it on the bank to rot. I don't know how that dog smelled it from so far away, but he went down there one night and had a high-heeled old time.

"Next morning he came wagging up, proud as punch, smelling like something that ought to be hauled away and buried, with his fur covered with loose gar scales. I peppered him with the BB gun till he went off down the pasture. Kept having to do that for several days before he was fit for human company. Can't have a dog running off customers." She heaved herself out of the chair.

"Speaking of which, there comes Miss Sudie, and I haven't finished sacking her order. Skunks! I haven't figured out why the good Lord created them—or mosquitoes—or water moccasins. Everything else I can kind of understand. Even you, Sol." The screen door creaked open and slammed shut behind her.

Sol was laughing silently, wiping his eyes on his blue bandana. He'd seldom had such a reaction from Mrs. Bragg in all his years of tale-telling on her porch.

The five little boys rose and set their bottles neatly in

their wooden crate. Will Henry grinned at Uncle Sol. "You really got her goin', this time," he said, as he hopped off the porch.

As Sol watched the boys straggle away down the road toward whatever summer adventure awaited them, he laughed again. Who'd have thought it would take *skunk* stories to get Letitia so wound up? He'd have to find some more, even if it took making them up out of the whole cloth.

I was the unlucky hay baling worker who had the skink run up my pants leg. If it had been a snake, I'd have been out of my jeans, hayfield full of men or not.

SNAKES IN THE HAYFIELD

It was midsummer, and the road was dusty with passing pickups and trailers loaded with bales of fragrant hay. Some of those pulled up along the pine-shaded track along the front of the little store or into the shadow cast by Mrs. Bragg's chinaberry tree, allowing their sweaty, dust-coated hay hands to buy a cold drink and perhaps a Moon Pie or a candy bar.

Solomon Peat, used to more than seventy years of East Texas summers, sat on the porch as usual, watching everything that went on. From time to time one of the hay hands would stop for a moment and greet him. He had entertained two generations of small boys with his stories, right there on that very porch, and none of them ever forgot him.

At noon he went inside and bought cheese and crackers from Mrs. Bragg, for it was too hot to walk a mile back up the road to his house. When he came outside again, he could see three of his usual five small boys clustered under the chinaberry tree, shooting red wasps with a BB gun. When he called them up to get their quarters for pop, they came without any prompting.

"Mr. Rogers has just about finished baling this cutting of hay," Will Henry said, as he plopped onto the edge of the porch with his frosty bottle. "Dad says it's been a good year...most good enough to make him wish he hadn't quit raising cattle. Chuck and Tim and me been riding along with the hands to open gates and such, but they're so near done they let us go."

Sol grunted and leaned his chair back against the wall. "I spent many a long hot day in the hayfield," he said, "when I was about your size and bigger. My Pa used to bale with one of the old-style balers that was run by a mule walkin' round and round at the end of a long arm that moved the works that compressed the hay.

"When I was little I used to tie out the bales. The blocks that dropped into the baler to separate the bales had holes in 'em, and when a block would push into sight along the square chute that formed the bales I'd poke a pair of wires through from one side, run around real quick and poke 'em back, then twist 'em together, top and bottom. Time the bale squeezed out the end of the chute, I'd have tied out another bale.

"Wasn't a bad job unless one of the hay pitchers didn't hear me when I yelled, 'Bale!' and kept forkin' in hay. That'd run the bale too long for the wires, and everything would come to a halt till I could piece together another bit of wire to make things match up."

Chuck, in his usual deliberate way, was squinting his eyes as he tried to visualize the system. "You mean the baler stayed in the same place, with that mule goin' round and round all the time?"

"Oh, he'd get a rest now and again. Somebody'd ride him down to the creek for a drink and we'd let him graze while we ate our dinner. But most of the time he'd just walk. And I think he slept a lot—seemed as if he'd wake up with a jump when you spoke to him.

"The other mule was hitched to the hay rake, and one or another of the hands kept rakin' up piles of hay for the men to fork into the baler. Worked pretty good, though not nearly as fast as these big balers that go down the windrows, gobblin' up hay and spittin' out bales like some kind of prehistoric monsters.

"Course, there was always snakes in the hayfields. Plenty of field mice and rabbits and such denned up there, not knowin' that their homes would get messed up before summer was over. Coachwhips and chicken snakes and blue racers slid through the grass huntin' 'em, too.

"I was walkin' across the big field once in hip-high grass, when I stepped down, looked down beside my foot, and near about jumped out of my skin. Right beside my bare foot was a coiled-up serpent, what kind I never stopped to inquire. I must've broke the standin' broad jump record of all time.

"So there was no shortage of critters to get themselves tangled up in our business. We'd be balin' away, when one of the fork hands'd yell and a snake that had been raked up into the pile would slither out of his forkfull, and we'd all jump everywhichaway.

"We had a dog when I was young that killed snakes like crazy. He'd go to the field with us and every time he found one he'd grab it crossways in his teeth. Then he'd shake his head hard enough to snap the critter's spine.

"Once we was balin' and he found a coachwhip. He got so enthusiastic he flung it about thirty feet up into the air. You talk about hay hands scrambling out of the way! Nobody wanted that thing for a necklace, I can tell you!"

Chuck hiccupped into his pop bottle, and Will Henry jogged him with an elbow. "Did they ever get baled up in the bales?" he asked.

Sol nodded. "Oftentimes I've pulled a bale out of the stack in the middle of the winter and there'd be half a dried-up snake danglin' out. Or we'd find his skeleton when the cows finished eatin' up the bale. We kept our eyes peeled, you better believe, for no matter what they say about non-poisonous snakes, there's been many a farmer die of blood poisoning after bein' bit by one that the experts say is safe."

Mrs. Bragg's deep voice rumbled inside the store, "My brother-in-law Todd Lucas died that way. Got bit by a chicken snake, thought nothin' of it, and was dead before they realized that bite had gone bad. If they'd gone for a tetanus shot, the doctor told Maudie, he'd never have had any problem."

Sol nodded. "Been more than one was took that way. So we kept our wits about us, when it came to watchin' out for slithery critters around the baler.

"The time I'm thinkin' about was a mighty hot day, with little puffy clouds threatenin' to turn into showers to wet our hay, so we were workin' at top speed. Ma was drivin' a wagon we borrowed from a neighbor, and one of my girl cousins was drivin' the other, comin' and goin' all the time as they loaded up and carried the hay over the hill to the big barn.

"When we had to go to the bushes, we had to be

mighty careful, 'cause there was likely to be womenfolks where you least expected 'em to be. Bein' small, I didn't worry as much about that as the grown fellers did, however. No, I kept tyin' out bales, gettin' my glove fingers tangled up and havin' to unwind myself, but keepin' up with the flow of hay pretty good. Nobody ever fussed at one of us boys, if we was doin' the best we could, so we didn't mind the work so much.

"I'd just seen a long black tail danglin' out of a bale that I'd tied out, so I had snakes pretty well on my mind. All of a sudden I felt somethin' wiggle at my ankle. Then it wiggled in my pants leg. Then it wiggled up at my waist."

Will Henry leaned forward. "You had a snake up your pants?" he asked in a horrified tone.

"That was what I intended to find out. I'd jumped a foot in the air when I felt the first wiggle, and by the time I hit the ground I was skinnin' off my pants. Girls or no girls, I didn't intend to stay confined in the same set of clothes with whatever it was that had run up my leg.

"Sure enough, the pants hit the ground and a blue racer took off like a skyrocket, if skyrockets went sideways. Cousin Carrie let out a yelp, and Ma turned the wagon she was drivin' and came hurryin'. Till then I didn't realize I was yellin' at the top of my lungs.

"Pa and the other hands seemed to be doin' some fancy footwork, too, and I knew we'd piled up a whole bunch of snakes in that last rake-full of hay. Time I came to myself, I was on top of the baler in my old drawers with holes in 'em, ducked down so the arm could go over my head. That mule never missed a step, and I doubt he even heard my yell.

"Ma got the mule stopped—she had to wake him up to do that—and by that time Pa and the others had themselves together enough to pretend they'd just been tryin' to stamp on snakes, instead of tryin' to get away from them. Ma just grinned and went back to haulin' hay.

"I put my pants back on, though I didn't really like to recall that a snake had been inside 'em last. We'd just about finished that field, by then, and nobody suggested we keep balin' by moonlight. Worse snakes than blue racers get out and hunt in the dark."

Chuck gulped the last of his strawberry pop and belched, hiding it politely behind his hand. Will Henry nodded thoughtfully. Mrs. Bragg was laughing quietly inside the store, and they all knew she was envisioning Solomon Peat as a boy shedding his trousers in a field full of girls.

"That'll give her a chuckle for a good long time to come," he whispered. "Never knew Letitia had it in her to think that was funny." The row of small boys grinned as they hopped down from the porch. It was funny, that was all, and they knew it.

I also was the one to bloody my neighbor's nose, for very similar reasons Mrs. Bragg tells about.

THE NOSE-BANGER

For once in his life, Solomon Peat was quiet as a dead turtle. Will Henry, Chuck, Tim, Les, and Fane were perched like sparrows along the edge of the porch of Mrs. Bragg's store, their eyes wide and their mouths firmly shut. Not one of them had ever seen Letitia Bragg truly and entirely furious before; that was enough to silence anybody.

She had chased Oliver Tweed out of the store so fast he had flown off the porch without using the steps. Now his old Ford pickup was tearing away up the road toward Possum Creek, leaving a storm of dust behind it, while she stood on the top step, her substantial bosom heaving, her race red, her fists clenched.

Only when she turned and sank into her chair did Sol dare to speak. "Letitia, I never knowed you to get so mad. What did that fellow do?"

"Never you mind!" she snapped. "If he ever comes back into my place of business, I'll get the shotgun out from under the counter and blow his head off. Mark you,

Solomon Peat, I mean it, and if you see him around you'd better pass the word."

Uncle Sol nodded meekly and took another chew of tobacco. The boys, their lips red-rimmed with strawberry pop, didn't move or speak. When somebody like Mrs. Bragg was riled up, it was best to keep your head down and your guard up.

After a while the angry snorts emanating from Mrs. Bragg's old rocker gentled down to deep breaths, then to her normal breathing. She leaned back and crossed her ankles and stared out across the pines toward the distant river.

After an even longer while, she said, "Sol, you think you're the only one's got a story to tell. You think you're the only one ever got mad enough to kill. I happen to have a temper, if you never noticed it, and once I came near to killing somebody, too."

Sol's eyes went wide. However, the old fellow knew how to tweak a story out of anyone who had one to tell. Inquiring silence, he had found, worked better than any question you could ask. Now he simply settled back to listen, and as if that pushed a button, Mrs. Bragg began to speak.

"When I was young and our children were about ten and four, Kenneth and I moved over to the other side of Templeton onto a place we bought from the Mortons, who had bought it from an old couple who'd lived there all their lives, until they went into a nursing home. The new owners sold us the house, which was the original farmhouse that was built before the turn of the century, with a few acres for a garden and livestock. They took the lower acreage down toward the creek and built a new house down there.

"We were both working hard, Ken in a lumberyard and me at the dry goods store in town. We left early and got home late, and when we were there we were up to our necks in work, trying to clean up forty years of dirt and repairing shackledy sheds and leaky roofs. But we were young and lively, and nothing fazed us, then." For an instant she looked almost young, remembering.

"Turned out the wife down the hill was crazy as a coot. She used to come sashaying up the hill when Ken was out cutting weeds or fixing the roof on the well house, and stand around in his way, flirting fit to kill. I'd usually have supper on cooking and couldn't come out and help him.

"She kept that up all summer and fall, until Ken bought enough barbed wire and posts to put up a fence between our house and theirs. It was pretty skimpy, because we hadn't much money, but barbed wire does a good job of keeping people on the right side of a fence.

"One afternoon I got home from work and looked over at the fence, and by heaven that silly idiot had tied their stallion to the top wire. If that horse had leaned forward for a bite of grass, he'd have snapped the wire and sliced himself into cutlets. About the time I got my clothes changed, Ken came in from work, and I told him, 'That woman has their horse tied to the fence. You'd better go out and tie the rope to the apple tree before he cuts himself to pieces.'

"Ken went right out and changed the rope over; it was all of about ten feet from the fence to a tree, and anybody but a fool would have used the tree to start with. Before he could get inside and change his shoes, that woman came flying up the hill and untied the rope, fastening it to the fence again. I saw Ken go red in the face, and I knew he was angry." Mrs. Bragg was looking pretty angry, herself, just remembering.

Sol looked sideways at the little boys, who seemed enthralled by hearing a story from Mrs. Bragg. This was a first in their lives, and they were soaking in every word.

She heaved a long sigh and leaned back again. "For once I didn't have my hands in something I couldn't turn loose of, so I slipped on my yard shoes and went out on the porch, some ten or twelve feet from where Ken was leaning over to untie that dratted rope again.

"He bent over, and that woman reached over the fence and started beating on his back with her fists. I swear, Sol, I didn't know I'd moved. One instant I was standing on the porch, the next my fist was sinking into Vinnie Nelson's nose."

Sol's chair legs hit the floor with a thump and he dropped his snuff can of spit, luckily before he had taken the top off. Will Henry gave a gulp, and Chuck almost fell off the porch. The other three boys were as still as fawns, waiting to learn what happened next.

"I never felt anything as purely *satisfying* as that nose going *crunch* under my fist," Mrs. Bragg said in a strangely soft voice. "Vinnie staggered backward and I felt myself getting ready to jump over the fence and finish her off, but Ken caught me by the elbows and lifted my feet off the ground. If he hadn't I'd likely have pounded that woman into the dust permanently.

"By the time he let me down, I'd cooled off a bit. Vinnie was standing there mopping her bleeding nose and staring at me like I was a bear, which wasn't far wrong, right at that particular moment. She moved the rope to the tree without a quibble, and that's the last time we ever spoke, though she used to stick her tongue out at us when we passed on the road."

Sol gave a grunt of laughter. "A grown woman? Stuck her tongue out? What kind of critter was she?"

Mrs. Bragg shook her grizzled head. "She was crazy, just like I said. A few years later her husband and sons moved off to California and left her sitting high and dry in her new house. I think she eventually got hauled off to a mental home."

The boys sighed, a soft sound like breeze through dried leaves, but they said nothing. It seemed there was still more to come, and they didn't intend to miss a word of the story.

"When she trudged off down the hill, Ken took my hand and we headed into the house to cook supper. I stepped into the living room, which had a big window looking out over the fence and the fields beyond it, and both my boys were standing there looking at me with big wide eyes and their mouths open.

"Don said, 'Mama, you did that just like a professional!' and little Cory nodded. That was the first time in my life I was ever proud of doing something so undignified as that. Still, anything that could make my sons look at me that way, plumb awe-struck, was satisfying. Mighty satisfying. They respected me in a little different way from that time on. Still do.

"The last time I saw Don, which was Christmas before last, I asked him if he remembered my hitting our neighbor, in fact. His eyes got big, just like they had when he was little, and he said, 'Mama, I never saw even Sugar Ray Robinson throw a better punch.'"

Solomon nodded. "I can see that, Letitia. I can surely see that. Boys don't often think of their mamas fighting to protect their daddies, but that happens, too. Fact is, it makes me think even more of you than I did to start with. A woman who can do something like that and admit it and not be ashamed of it for all the wrong reasons is a woman to treasure."

Mrs. Bragg blushed. Actually blushed, not red and angry as she had looked before, but a bit rosy and bashful, as if she didn't know how to handle a compliment.

"Well, Ken was never ashamed of that. He bragged about it to the fellows at the lumber mill, in fact. And he wouldn't let me think of it as being unladylike. He never had much patience with women who were so ladylike they weren't worth the powder and lead to blow them sky high, anyway.

"No, I can't say I ever regretted bloodying her nose, though I feel kind of sorry for Vinnie now. She had to have been mighty unhappy to run her family off the way she did."

She rose from her creaky rocker to go inside again, but Will Henry stopped her. "Mrs. Bragg," he asked in an awed voice, "would you give me your *autograph*?" He pulled from his pocket a tattered little notebook with a chewed pencil stub tied to it with string.

"And sign a page for me—and me—and me—and me!" the other boys chimed in.

Now she blushed even more brightly, but she signed. Oh yes, Letitia Bragg proudly signed the very first autographs anybody had ever asked her for in all her busy and useful life.

And Uncle Sol, watching quietly from his chair,

smiled. When she finished with the notebook, he pulled out his wallet and held out a scrap of paper of his own. "I've got to have the signature of the champeen boxer of Cotton County, too," he said.

"Oh, Sol, you old fool!" she said. But she signed that, too, before she clumped into the store and slammed the screen door behind her.

That cow's name was Rosa, and she was, in a way, my role model, as I was undersized, too. She taught me that nobody was big enough to bully me, either.

THE CROOKED-TAIL COW

Solomon Peat usually walked slowly down the road to the store at Possum Creek, taking his time and enjoying everything that moved along the way. He didn't miss a crow circling high in the polished October sky or a squirrel scampering up a hickory tree with nuts in its cheeks. The distant scree of a hawk told him the predator was circling over Mrs. Hawks's chicken pen, and even at this time of morning he could hear bobcats quarrelling as they made their way to their dens.

Much of his long life had been lived here in the river bottoms, and Sol could read the sounds and signs around him better than anyone left alive, except for one or two of the old black fishermen who made their homes down on the banks of the Nichayac River.

The years he had spent managing lumber mills in Tompkins and Templeton couldn't erase the instincts sharpened by his youthful ramblings through the big woods. That was why he picked up the vibration under the soles of his boots in time to jump into the bushes. Somebody was driving a herd of cows out of the bottomlands along the river, taking them to higher pastures for the winter. Getting trampled by a bunch of cows was not Sol's idea of a good time, and he felt a bit disgruntled at having his morning meander disrupted.

Before long the first, a yearling heifer, appeared around the bend ahead, her head up, her crooked tail swishing with irritation. She was black as midnight, and behind her came an entire herd of dark-colored yearlings, all Jerseys. Sol nodded. This was Sammy Deal's bunch that had been fattening in the bottoms, all of them descendants of a single black cow from a famous registered herd in Louisiana.

Lord knows, he thought, I know about those. My Cousin Betty and her man had one of the first to come into East Texas. Thinking about that oddball critter, he waited out the dusty passage of the herd and trudged on to Mrs. Bragg's store, where he dropped into his hickory splint chair and sighed hugely.

Being as it was October, none of his usual audience of small boys was waiting on the porch, but there was a salesman there, drinking Coca-Cola, two of the old ladies who bartered fresh eggs for part of their groceries, and Letitia Bragg herself. All were ranged along the wall, sitting in an assortment of rickety chairs taken out of the store, enjoying the bright, cool weather.

Mrs. Bragg was frowning as she fanned the remnant of dust away from her face. "I swear, Sol, it's a nuisance every time they take those cattle past here. A car is bad enough, but it's only got four wheels and the dust settles pretty soon. Cows, though, stir up a storm, and before they've all gone past there's manure mixed up with the dust, as well. Those black cows seem like they kick up more than any other kind, too."

"That's because they have those little bitty hooves and they walk so fast," Sol said, settling his chair back against the wall behind him.

"Now what would you know about cows, Solomon Peat?" she asked him, sounding impatient. "Except for a while when you were young, you never ran a dairy in your life."

Sol peered at her through the last remnant of dust. "Letitia, my Cousin Betty and her husband Bradley had one of them black Louisiana cows in their herd. Called her Rosa.

"She was a little bitty thing, and her tail, like almost all her breed's, was crooked at a right angle about halfway down its length. She could catch you the most godawful swat with that thing. Seemed as if the angle gave her more power when she switched her tail to her left. I remember putting the milker on her once, and when I turned to get onto my feet she whipped me across the face so hard it bled."

Mrs. Bragg sighed. For fifteen years she'd been trying to catch Sol out on some of his tales. Every last time, except for the most outrageous stories that he winked at himself, he was able to offer witnesses to prove that those wild occurrences had actually happened. It was downright discouraging to her, and Sol knew that with wicked delight.

"I'd think a small animal like that would be bullied by the other cows," said the catfish man, who had finished his Coke and was rising to go on about his route.

Sol let him get out of sight before he laughed, being

naturally polite to suffering salesmen who had just had to deal with Mrs. Bragg. Then he let out a guffaw.

"I never saw a cow big enough to bully Rosa. She weighed maybe six hundred pounds, while the rest of Betty's bunch was right up there at a thousand or more, but not one of 'em ever tried to mess with Rosa but once. She'd take a run at 'em and butt 'em amidships till they lost their interest messin' with her.

"In summer, Betty told me, she waited in the shade until her time to be milked. Then she came across that cowlot as straight as if a surveyor laid out a line, and anything got in her way got butted out of it. Finally got so when Rosa began to move, all those great big lummoxes of Holsteins and such just began to move in self defense."

"I can't see how...," Mrs. Bragg began, but Sol shook his head.

"Letitia, you and I both know people that wouldn't make a good washing of soap but who can bulldoze their way through anything that comes along. That was Rosa. It was the look in her eye as much as anything else. Self-confidence—that was her secret. She never doubted for one minute that she could handle anything on four legs—or two, for that matter—and that meant she could.

"Not that she was mean, but you didn't mess with her. Tend to business and do your work and she never raised a hoof or made a problem—except with that dratted tail, of course, but that was because of the flies that were bitin' her.

"People kept tellin' Bradley he ought to get rid of her. Such a little cow couldn't give much milk, they said. He just grinned and kept milkin' her. She ate about half what one of the big 'uns did and gave just about as much milk, as I can swear to. I had to milk her by hand, one night while I was there helpin' out. Lights went out, and we had to milk the whole bunch by hand, actually. Time we got done it was almost time to start over again."

He looked down at his liver-spotted hands and sighed. "Back then I could mighty nigh squeeze a stick of stovewood in two, I had such a grip. Came from milkin' our cow at home, from the time I was a tad. Now it's all I can do to scratch myself, and not to do much good, then."

He chuckled again. "Funny thing happened, the year after I was out there. I went back for a visit with Yale and Ma, and Betty had somethin' strange tacked to the front wall of the hay barn. It looked somethin' like a whip, with a tassel on the end.

"I went up and looked it over real good, and it looked mighty familiar, but I couldn't quite decide why. Betty came out with Ma, after a while, and she started laughin' fit to kill.

"'Sol,' she said, 'I'd've thought you'd know that tail anyplace. It's Rosa's.'

"I felt kind of sad, because I'd liked that little cow. "'When did she die?' I asked her.

"'Oh, she's not dead,' Betty said. 'She's still as feisty as ever. She just came up one night to be milked and her tail had snapped off right at the bend. We doctored the stub and bandaged it and thought no more about it.

"'A few months later, Brad was out in the woods lookin' for a cow with a new calf. And there, wrapped around a tree where she'd given one of her patented whiplash tail switches, was Rosa's tail, which had whipped so hard around a sweetgum saplin' that when she started to leave it just snapped the lower part right off.'"

He sighed. "That made me feel sorry for that cow. Being black, she was the one flies made for first and most. White cows they didn't bother so bad. Why, black and white Holsteins would have patches of flies on their black spots and only one of two on the white. Poor Rosa, being black from head to tail, must be bein' eaten alive, I thought.

"But when I asked Betty, she grinned. 'We soaked a piece of tow-sack in oil and tied it onto her stub,' she told me. 'It works better than her own tail did. She never could flap her right side very well, but now she can work both sides over.'

"I went out, after a while, when the cows were coming up for the evenin' milkin', and sure enough there was Rosa, waitin' in the shade, whiskin' that tow-sack tail back and forth and waitin' to bulldoze her way to the barn, when her turn came. Made me feel a lot better, I can tell you."

One of the old ladies stared at the road where dabs of cow manure still marked the passing of the herd. "I noticed that a lot of those animals had crooked tails. Must run in the breed, I suppose."

Sol nodded. "Every black Jersey in this part of the state is descended from one prize cow back maybe sixty years ago. Rosa was her own calf, but those now must be a long way down the family tree. Most still have crooked tails, too. Some say that's because the original stock was bred over in Louisiana, pastured at a sharp bend in the road. Course, I think that may be just superstition, but you never know."

The dust was gone now, and the old ladies rose to make their way back home. "I think I'll take the path through the woods," Mrs. Wilkerson said. "I don't want to step in more cow-dabs than I have to."

Mrs. Patton gave a gulp of laughter. "Makes me think of my Uncle Sawyer," she choked. "He come home drunk before daylight one mornin' and dropped his hat in the cow-lot. Tried on four before he got the right one."

Sol bent double. Mrs. Bragg, often slow to catch on, frowned. Then she began to grin. "You mean he tried on *cowpats*, thinking they were his hat? Must have looked awful, before he was through."

Mrs. Patton's boot-button eyes were gleaming with tears of laughter. "Mama said he looked like he'd wallowed through that lot. Grandma had to put him in the horse trough and scrub him with lye soap before he was fit for human company again."

She rose and followed her companion down the steps. Both turned into the woods path and soon disappeared into the trees.

Sol chuckled. "Well, she topped my tale, for once. I swear I'd have loved to see that drunk idiot, out there tryin' on hats."

Mrs. Bragg snorted, but turned it into a sneeze. More than one laugh at one story went against her principles.

*My Dad sold Levi Garret Snuff during the Depression.
Though he spoke meticulous English (with a Mississippi
accent) he knew he must not intimidate his customers, so
he could adapt his conversation to the speaking style of
those with whom he was working.*

UNCLE SOL AND THE ENGLISH LANGUAGE

A bunch of fishermen from Templeton had descended
upon Possum Creek, on their way to the big lake. They
were equipped with about a thousand dollars worth of gear
each, Sol thought, and they'd come back with about fifteen
cents worth of fish. Still, it was such business that kept
Mrs. Bragg's store going, and he was set to ignore this
batch after he howdied them as they passed.

The last man, however, turned and held out his hand.
"Solomon Peat!" he said. "I haven't seen you in *years*!"

Sol peered at him and began to grin. "Professor Tim
Jonas! By golly, I'd have thought you'd be pushin' up daisies by now. It's been—my goodness, it must be forty
years since I finished at the college, and you were no
spring chicken then. Neither was I, if truth be told, but the
mill owners paid for my education, after I'd been runnin'
the thing for years. Figured if I was to deal with their buy-

ers, I'd better know a lot more than I got in the country school out here."

Jonas let his companions go on into the store. He pulled Mrs. Bragg's rocker across the entryway and plopped into it to sit beside Sol. "They knew they had a bright one, Sol," he said. "I never taught anybody who caught on any faster than you did. When you first came into class, with your country accent, I thought you would have a hard time, but by golly it turned out that you *knew* English grammar, you just didn't *use* it."

Sol nodded. "Miz Kinsey, who taught me in the eighth grade, made sure and certain that her students learned grammar and punctuation and spelling. You stayed in her class till you got it. One of my classmates was nineteen before he ever got out of eighth grade, and then he had to go to work. But by then he knew English grammar or he'd have stayed there till he died of old age."

Jonas leaned back in the rocker and guffawed. Wiping his eyes with a blue bandana, he said, "I do wish schools still ran that way. Before I retired, a couple of years ago, we were getting young people who had graduated from big schools, and they had to be taught to read before we could teach them anything else. We had to set aside a big area in the library where students could teach other students to read."

Sol sighed. "Our little old school, way out here in the bottomlands, got gobbled up by the bigger one at Grange, halfway to Templeton. Since then the young'uns have to ride a bus for a couple of hours every day, which is a pure waste, and they don't learn near as much as Miss Brooks used to teach 'em right here at home."

One of the fishermen emerged from the store and

dropped onto a crate to drink his Coke. He looked at Sol with considerable disdain, and the old man knew just exactly what he was thinking. *This is an old codger who never stirred out of the boondocks and couldn't out-think a wood-tick.* That was what he was thinking.

Sol looked at Tim Jonas, who rose and said, "I think I'll go get something to drink, too. Sol, this is Professor Finley, who teaches philosophy. You may find him interesting."

Finley gave a refined snort, and that set Sol off. "So, Professor," he said in his most elegant English, "What is your position on science versus art as a defining principle of reality?"

Finley choked on his cold drink, but he rallied. "I can't say that I have much respect for art," he said. "It's science that measures and analyzes. Art just plays with emotions and subjective perceptions."

Sol shook his head, as if saddened by this news. "I am afraid that I agree with Henri Bergson, the French philosopher. His belief, and I am afraid I share it, is that science uses intelligence to create symbols that are supposed to describe reality but that actually falsify it. He believed that art, being based on intuition unaided by intellect, cuts through conventional symbols and beliefs and makes one face reality itself."

Finley was saved by the emergence of his fellows from the store. He rose with enthusiasm and jumped off the porch. "An interesting hypothesis," he said to Sol. "Too bad there isn't time to discuss it further."

But as Jonas led him away, Sol heard the professor mutter to him, "Who is this old fellow, anyway?"

Sol knew that Tim Jonas would lead him a long way

up the garden path before he ever told him about Sol's college days—if he ever enlightened him at all. Tim had a wicked sense of humor, or he'd never have sicced Sol on the luckless philosopher in the first place.

The fishermen piled into their pickups and pulled away, with their boat trailers bumping along behind. Mrs. Bragg came out of the store and dropped into the rocker.

"Sol," she said, "you always manage to amaze me. That arrogant...*creature*...had just been in MY store, patronizing ME as if I were some ignorant countrywoman who couldn't find her backside with both hands and a road map. He went out there to do the same to you—I could see it on his face.

"But you pulled the rug right out from under him, as neatly as I ever heard it done. It isn't often that I pay anybody a compliment—you know that better than most. But I have to give praise where praise is due. You knocked him off his pins, Solomon Peat, and it's plain somebody needed to do that a long time ago."

Sol blushed—he could feel the blood warming his cheeks, and it had been a few decades since THAT had happened to him. To get such a compliment from Letitia Bragg was a feat few had ever accomplished.

"Well, I tell you, Letitia," he said in his most serious tone, "some people get too big for their britches early and never get over it. I felt it was time to show that sapsucker that there are things in heaven and earth that HIS philosophy never dreamed of, sure enough."

Mrs. Bragg nodded and stared off toward the river, where a thin trail of dust still marked the passage of the convoy of professorial fishermen.

"Jonas did that on purpose," she noted in a casual tone.

"You knew that, I take it?"

"Oh yes," Sol replied. "Tim gave me a wink before he left the porch, so I knew what to expect. Tim and me, we got along mighty well, while he taught me English."

Letitia Bragg sighed deeply. "I just wish they gave courses in courtesy and common sense at that university," she said. "But they'd have to hire a few new teachers, if they did."

"Aaaamen!" said Solomon Peat.

My friend James Choron grew up in Shelby County, Texas, and his family knew all the old timers living out in the woods of that area. He told me the story of this elderly deacon who protected his church to the bitter end.

THE DEACON

The Methodists were having a big preaching up between Possum Creek and Grange, at their weather-beaten church, and the Bishop was coming to town, if you could call Possum Creek a town. The new part-time preacher, Fred Monroe, was all agog over that, for he had only been serving the congregation for a few months.

He drove his old Dodge from house to house to invite everybody to the event, even if they happened to be Baptist or Catholic. In a place that small, you needed every warm body you could muster.

He came to Mrs. Bragg's store near the last, which was bright of him. He knew he could sit on the porch and drink a long, cold soda pop and cool off after his efforts. He looked forward to visiting with Solomon Peat, too. Of all the preachers the hamlet ever had, Monroe was the only one who enjoyed the old fellow's tales.

He plopped down into Mrs. Bragg's rocker, holding a

dripping bottle of Pepsi, just dredged out of the icy water of the old fashioned cooler, and grinned at Sol. "We're going to have a wonderful time next week when the Bishop gets here. You ought to come and help us celebrate, Mr. Peat," he said.

Sol spat into his snuff can and returned it to his overalls pocket. "Sounds as if you intend to put the big pot in the little pot," he replied. "Never been much for churches, though. Particularly since they shut down all the little bitty ones out in the woods and sucked their folks into the town churches. You've got one of the very few left, Mr. Monroe, and I hope you appreciate it."

Monroe took a long sip and cocked his head thoughtfully. "I can see that the old folks, way out in the boondocks, might object to having to drive ten miles to church," he said. "But you have to admit that a bigger church has more amenities."

Solomon cocked his chair against the wall and looked out across the pine woods. "You ever hear the tale about old Deacon Highsmith?" he asked. "Belonged to Praise Be the Kingdom Church, down where Dogwood Knob used to be. They had a congregation of about ten, until six of 'em died over a couple of years, back when I was a boy. About that time the Methodist Church reorganized the way it did business and started shuttin' down the little ones like Praise Be."

Monroe nodded. That was part of the history of the church, and he had studied about it at seminary.

Sol closed his eyes, as if looking into the past. "Old Deacon Highsmith was about ninety-two, when that happened. Wore stovepipe britches and a swallow-tail coat, a tall black hat, and carried a brass-headed walking cane.

Rode a big black horse you wouldn't have thought he could climb up on, much less control.

"The Deacon was a tall man, with whiskers down to his belt buckle, and Pa said he had eyes that seemed able to stare a hole through a stone wall, black and deep-sunk and sort of wild lookin'. My Pa said that when Highsmith heard about shuttin' down his church he turned plumb white.

"Said, 'No way they're goin' to shut me out of the Lord's house. Take word up to Templeton that this is my last word.'"

Five little boys, two white and three black, approached the porch hopefully, and Sol pulled a handful of quarters out of his pocket. "Go get you some pop, boys. Then be quiet. I'm tellin' Mr. Monroe a story about his church."

They trooped into the store, and Sol sank back and ruffled his thick white eyebrows. "Nobody fooled with Mr. Ned Highsmith, Pa said, because when he said somethin' he meant it right down to his boot-heels. One of the members carried the word to Templeton, and the District Supervisor was there when he told the preacher the news.

"The preacher, who held services down at Praise Be the Kingdom every third Sunday—sort of like you do with your church, would've let it drop, right then and there. He knew Ned Highsmith, and he understood that only when the old man was six foot under would that little church close its doors.

"The District Supervisor, on the other hand, had come down to East Texas from the city, and he didn't understand what he was about to deal with. He held a meetin' about church affairs, and before it broke up he told Preacher Dickson he intended just to go down to Dogwood

Knob early the next morning and take all the paperwork out of the church. Then it would be closed, officially, and nobody could do a thing about it."

Sol spat thoughtfully and sighed. "Nobody's ever figured out how news travels so fast down here in the woods. There was no telephones, back then, and no cars. In fact the Supervisor, Mr. Cutworth, had to start at three A.M. in his buggy, behind a good stout gelding, to get down to Dogwood Knob about dawn.

"Now, this wasn't the usual sort of job for somebody of his standing in the church, but he felt it was his duty. Nobody could get away with having his own way in opposition to church policy. So Cutworth dragged himself out of bed and set off in a drizzling rain to seize the papers. The gelding was pretty miserable, the road was worse, and by the time Cutworth could see a line of gray along the east, beyond the little circle of yellow light from his lantern, he was just about as miserable as both.

"Still, he was doin' the Lord's work, he was certain. He came sloppin' around the last bend in the muddy road, just about the time it was daylight. But when he pulled up at the long flight of steps that led up into the building, he saw a big black horse hitched to the hitching rail."

Monroe leaned forward. The five boys, now equipped with cold bottles, listened with full attention. Even Mrs. Bragg, just inside the screen door, was breathing hard as she eavesdropped.

"It was still pretty dim, what with the rain and all, and Cutworth leaned out of the buggy, tryin' to see if anybody was there. Surely a man of ninety-two wouldn't be out so early in such weather! But he was. At the top of the steps, under the dinky little eaves, there was a lanky black shape that stood up and up and up till it seemed to be ten feet tall, countin' the black hat.

"'Mr. Cutworth,' came a rumbling voice, 'I told 'em to tell you that this church ain't a-shutting down. I meant it. If you start to climb these steps, you may get to the first and maybe the second, but by the time you reach the third you're goin' to have a bullet in your gizzard.'

"Cutworth told my Pa, years and years later, that he never would feel nearer to his Maker than he did right then, because Highsmith was holding the biggest horse pistol he ever saw in his life. As the light got stronger, he could see the hammer was cocked, and the old man's finger was tight on the trigger.

"Still he was a man who tried to do his duty, so he said, 'Mr. Highsmith, if you kill me they'll come and put you in jail. You'll stand trial. Maybe hang.'

"Highsmith began to laugh. 'Man, I'm ninety-two years old. How long a sentence they goin' to give me? This point in my life, I can't see I've got anything at all to lose. So you just start up those steps and see how far you get.'

"Mr. Cutworth might be a dutiful man, but Pa said he was no fool. He looked at the black horse, which looked like it could have carried Death itself on the day of Armageddon. He looked up at Highsmith, who could have stood in for Death, right then and there.

"Then he hauled on the reins and got that buggy turned around and skedaddled out of there as fast as the horse would trot, after his long trip. When he got back to the big church in Templeton, the Supervisor went in and knelt down and thanked the Good Lord that he was still alive."

"What about the church?" The question came from

two directions, for Monroe and Letitia Bragg spoke at once.

Sol chuckled. "Ned Highsmith lived five years longer, just to spite Cutworth, Pa said. Only when he was well and truly planted did the Methodist church close Praise Be to the Kingdom. By then there was only two members, and they was too old and feeble, by then, to do more than fuss.

"They did a lot of that, though. Folks still talked about them when I was a boy."

Monroe finished his Pepsi and wiped his forehead on a snowy handkerchief. "Times have certainly changed," he said, his tone filled with gratitude.

Sol cocked an eye toward Mrs. Bragg, who was dimly visible through the screen door. "Just don't go gettin' crossways with your church members," he told the young minister. "Folks down here in the woods keep to their old habits pretty much, and you might find that Ned Highsmith's kind still flourishes down in the river bottoms and the pine thickets.

"Warn that Bishop, too. Tell him not to be too high and mighty, or some old codger may take a scunner at him and scare the living daylights out of him, like Ned did to Cutworth. I've seen it happen...."—Sol drew down his brows fiercely—"...Even in recent times. So take care, young Fred. Take care."

The preacher rose and placed his bottle neatly in the wooden case. Giving a nervous nod to Mrs. Bragg and a grin at the boys, he hopped down the steps to his car to set off on his rounds again.

Mrs. Bragg stepped outside and closed the screen gently behind her. "You just about scared that young man to death, Sol," she said, but her usual fire was not in her words. "Still, maybe it's a good thing. Make him careful, if nothing else."

Then she dropped into her rocker and gave a single deep grunt of laughter. Sol and the boys dissolved along with her.

Times had changed, maybe, but the people of Possum Creek still treasured their independence, whether religious or otherwise. That Bishop had better watch his step, Sol knew, as he watched the dust settle behind the retreating Dodge.

My sister told me this story—she lives a short distance from the site of Allie's misadventure and heard the account from those who saw it happen.

AN ALLIGATOR TALE

Solomon Peat sat on the porch of Mrs. Bragg's grocery store, his face red with the effort of climbing the steps. He was getting older, that was too true, and even Mrs. Bragg looked concerned as she brought him his usual strawberry pop.

"Sol, it's so hot you need to stay home and let Willa turn on the air conditioning. At your age, you're likely to have a stroke." She handed him a paper napkin to wipe his sweaty forehead.

"It was bad enough when I had to start drivin' the Chevy to the store," he protested. "I used to love my mornin' walk. Now the old legs don't mind me worth a hoot, but I don't intend to give up my visits with the folks down here. Even if my usual bunch of boys have got so big they're busy most of the time, there's other folks to talk to." He turned to watch a tan Ford stop under the chinaberry tree.

"There's Tad Johnson," he said. "He always liked to

hear my tales, when he was a little fellow."

"We all like to," Mrs. Bragg agreed, though a few years back that would have been an unthinkable admission for her to make. She looked sharply at Johnson as he climbed her steps and flopped into the splint chair beside Sol. "You look like the cat that ate the canary," she said to the young man.

"I've got a tale to tell that'll make Uncle Sol laugh," Johnson chuckled. "I thought of him right off after my cousin Jimmie called, this morning. You recall Jimmie's dairy farm, over toward Central Point?" he asked Sol.

"Seems I went over there a while back with my friend Jonah to pick up a cow he bought from Jimmie," the old man admitted. "Nice neat dairy barn, trim house, good-sized lake at the back of the meadow. He said they caught big bass out of the pond."

Johnson snorted with laughter. "That pond is almost the...I guess you'd call it the scene of the crime. Did he mention his alligator when you were there, Sol?"

Solomon Peat's faded blue eyes widened. "Alligator? No, we got to talkin' about bird dogs, and we never got around to discussin' the lake much."

"Well, they built that lake somethin' like twenty years back, and right off the dam started bein' cut into by nutria—you know, those critters they imported from Louisiana to raise for meat and fur. The dam had to be fixed every few months or all the water would leak into the creek.

"When little Roy was about four the family took a trip to Florida, and nothin' would do that boy but he had to have a live baby alligator. Which was fine as long as they could keep her in a washtub, but when she got too big for that and started chasin' the little dachshund all over the patio, they realized it was time for a change. So they took her down to the lake and turned her loose.

"Jimmie said you never saw nutria disappear so fast in all your life. They had a good solid dam and a fat alligator and a lot of fish. Of course, once the nutria got cleaned out, Allie (that's what they called her) got bored and ambled across the road to the Lamberts' cattle pond, which also had a bunch of nutria denned up in the dam. She'd meander from one body of water to the other, as her supply ran short, and things worked out fine for everybody, though nobody did much swimmin' in either pond."

"Now that I can believe," Mrs. Bragg interjected. "I've seen many a gator down here along the river, and not one of them ever made me want a closer acquaintance."

"So what was the crime?" asked Sol, leaning forward with his hands on his blue denim knees.

"You remember a few years back when they passed the Endangered Species Act?" Johnson glanced at both the older people, and they nodded. They remembered it all too well, for the river people had resented being required to leave gators alone, even when they posed a danger to fishing nets and lines, not to mention to the people who set them.

"It's plumb illegal to mess with an alligator, much less to abuse one," Tad chuckled. "But the law reckoned without old Miz Brackart. You ever know her, Sol?"

Solomon shook his head, but Letitia Bragg sat up straighter. "My cousin Ella used to live next door to her, past Central Point on the highway. Most meddlesome woman ever, she claimed. Stuck her nose into everybody's business and then yelled to high heaven if she found what she was looking for, which was mainly scandal and wrongdoing."

Johnson nodded. "That's the one. She's got meaner and more meddlesome, they tell me, and she's scared of mice and snakes and spiders and possums and goats and just about anything that isn't human. Some of those, too, of course.

"So last week when she took the back road to Templeton right past Jimmie's dairy, she found Allie, who was by then about fourteen feet long, moving across the middle of the road, peaceful as could be. The poor gator was just making her regular change of ponds, bothering nobody, but Miz Brackart couldn't be satisfied to stop her car and let the old girl cross the road in peace. No she had to use her car phone to call the sheriff's office and yell about a dangerous animal on the road."

"Sounds just like her," Mrs. Bragg grumbled. "She used to yell and scream about Ella's tomcat walking on top of their line fence, as if that was going to make the whole thing fall down. Threatened to sue Ella if the animal ever came over to do his business in her flower bed, too, but old Thomas was too smart to go near that woman."

Tad leaned back and stretched out his long legs. "The deputies weren't as smart as that tomcat. They came tearin' up, in about ten minutes, six cars of 'em, sirens going, lights blinking, and blocked off the road. Jimmie tells me they had somewhat of a rodeo, right there on the asphalt, trying to lasso old Allie, who didn't take kindly to being man-handled and hog-tied.

"By the time they got her roped, there must have been ten cars full of folks watching the show. No matter that Jimmie and his wife tried to talk 'em out of it, they hauled that poor creature into the back of a pickup, her tail all tied up in a loop, her jaws roped together, and her feet bound up.

"Jimmie called the sheriff's office and asked where they were taking her. Sheriff said out to the Taylor alligator farm, where they slaughter the gators they raise to sell for meat. Jimmie went into orbit, I tell you. His wife called the wildlife people and the Forest Service and everybody else she could think of. The folks at the college in Templeton got into the act, too, and things got hot for the sheriff's department.

"Turned out, as nobody can own a gator, they couldn't take Allie back to the farm, but those idiot deputies had to go out to the Taylor farm at Blackwater and find Allie. Luckily the owner knew all his own gators and could point out Allie without any problem.

"He refused to wade out among the big alligators, himself, though. Taylor told Jimmie he stood there and grinned like a possum while the deputies had to go out into the mess and kick hissing gators out of their way and go through all the hassle of roping Allie up again.

"This time they carried her to the river and dumped her in. So it turned out all right for Allie, who probably is already set up with a mate, and it left the deputies with egg all over their faces, which is just about right, the way I see it."

Solomon leaned his chair back against the wall and his round belly began to quiver. Then his jowls began to joggle. And then he erupted into an explosion of laughter. Mrs. Bragg and Tad were laughing, too, and the three sat there wiping their streaming eyes and guffawing.

When he could speak, Sol said, "I just know Willie

Phipps was one of the deputies, and Lon Forrest and Cory DePew were, too. Three of the dumbest men God ever put on this earth. I'd have loved to see 'em stompin' around among the gators, tryin' to catch a partic'lar one and tie her up, while the rest stood around and hissed at 'em."

Tad buried his face in his hands and began to whoop again. "Cory DePew slipped in the mud and gator mess and fell flat on his face, right under one of the critters," he finally managed to gasp. "Just about died of fright and messed himself up even more than the muck in the pen did.

"Jimmie got a first-hand account of the show from Hobe Taylor himself. Said Taylor could hardly talk, he kept getting so tickled.

"I'd bet if somebody else calls in an alligator scare, the sheriff's department is going to be mighty slow and careful about answering it. The Wildlife people just about took the skin off 'em for messing with Allie in the first place. Talked about suing the county for harassment of an endangered species. I'll bet Sheriff Skinner was steamed... he thinks he helped God hang the moon, anyway, and he resents being criticized by anybody, much less somebody higher up than he is in the pecking order."

Tad wiped his eyes and rose. "So, Uncle Sol, is that tale worth a strawberry pop, like you used to buy for me when I was little?"

"That's worth a round for everybody," Sol said, digging into his overalls pocket. "Even though they don't taste near as good out of that newfangled machine as they did out of the old cooler full of icy water. You, too, Letitia. Set 'em up all around."

The three sat on the porch as shadows stretched across

the dusty road and the sun sank behind the western rank of pines. The chilly cans felt good in their sweaty hands, and they looked at each other and grinned as a gator boomed, far away down in Sundown Swamp.

"Might be Allie herself," Sol murmured. "And that would be right poetic, wouldn't it?"

I remember seeing that ancient car with its hardly less ancient driver moving down the highway, his neck craning out of the window, passers-by almost driving into the ditch as they watched in fascination.

THE LOQUAT EYES

It was a cool autumn morning, and the air smelled like dust and falling leaves and the fall of the year. Solomon Peat inhaled deeply and then sighed. "Seems as if fall comes quicker every year," he said to Mrs. Bragg, "and I get creakier every year, too."

The storekeeper plopped into her worn rocker and looked about at those gathered on the porch of her general store. "I guess we all get creakier as time goes by," she said. "Sometimes I feel like the Wonderful One-Hoss Shay. Did you learn that verse when you were in school, Sol?"

Sol grinned. "Sure did, but I never appreciated it till the first time I saw Bud Hinkle drivin' along the dirt road in his old car. That was the darndest vehicle you ever saw, Letitia. I don't know if it was any known make of automobile, 'cause it was so old it still had kerosene lamps up front. Might have been one of them that folks used to cobble together in their barnyards."

Mrs. Bragg leaned forward and stared at him. "Solomon Peat! There hasn't been a car like that for sixty years or more!"

"Hasn't been one MADE, Letitia, but Old Bud drove his when I was a young man, and it was older than Methuselah even then. Looked like a buggy with a canvas flap top. Stood high up on little narrow tires, and those head lamps made it stand out real plain.

"I've seen strangers most run off the road, tryin' to see what it could be." He began to chuckle, his round belly joggling. "But when Bud was drivin' it, that was when things got interesting."

"I'd think anybody who'd drive something like that on a modern road was crazy," said one of the little boys perched along the edge of the porch. "Dad says old, slow cars are more dangerous than fast ones, these days."

"These days that's true, but when I first saw Bud out on the main highway, it was just a two-lane road with asphalt on the top. Nobody went much over fifty, because the road would buck you off into the ditch if you did. Bud did about twenty-five, maybe, which was strainin' his vehicle to its limits.

"What made the thing so memorable was Bud himself, though. He was, like you say, crazy. Not dangerous, of course, but odd, like most of the Hinkles. Their mama was a Loquat from down at Pine Ridge, and that bunch all had eyes that looked off into someplace else.

"Sometimes the rest of the person seemed to follow, too. They could get lost standing still in the middle of the road."

Mrs. Bragg leaned back, her eyes lighting up. "Was

that the fellow my dad used to tell me about?"

Sol nodded. "He was the one. Tall, skinny man. Had a neck like a goose. It seemed to have at least three Adam's apples, it was so long and stringy. When he got in his car, he was so tall his head couldn't fit down under the canvas top.

"He'd bend that long neck out of the window and stick his head up—came higher than the top. You'd be drivin' down the road, thinking, and round the bend would come Bud, cranin' out the window of that antique monstrosity. I've seen folks mighty near run off the road, while they tried to see what on earth was going on. Old Bud and his car just about made a match, I always thought. One old as creation and the other one way out in left field."

The boys snickered at the image, and Mrs. Bragg almost laughed. Not quite, but that was close enough to please Uncle Sol.

"Reminds me of that Studebaker you told us about, back a way," she said. "If you could locate that car, now...."

Solomon shook his head. "Wouldn't surprise me if they buried old Bud in that thing," he told her. "He drove it till he died, and nobody could manage to think of him without seein' him in it, chugging down the road, his big pale eyes lookin' off into eternity, seemed as if."

He looked up the road, where an aged pickup, all its color provided by a thick coat of rust, was wheezing and coughing its way toward the store. "I have to admit, though, it made that thing look like a Buick," he said.

Letitia Bragg's eyes narrowed. "That's Hemmy Wiggins, and she'll want credit. Always does. That woman! If she'd sell off a bit of timber or even some of her land she'd have enough money to live on, but no! Wants to leave it all to her children, who are a bunch of ungrateful rascals.

"You tend to her, will you, Sol? Maybe you can say no to her. I certainly can't!" Mrs. Bragg hopped off the end of the porch and disappeared around the end of the store before the pickup came near enough to detect her flight.

Sol coughed and stood. "You know I ain't much good at sayin' no, Letitia," he called after his old friend. "You also know I'll pay for her groceries. You are one sneaky woman, you know that?"

He followed the feeble old woman who got out of the pickup into the store, pulling his wallet from his pocket as he went. Then he had a sudden thought.

"Mrs. Wiggins, weren't you a Loquat before you married?" he asked.

She turned toward him, her wide, pale eyes seeming to look either through or past him. She gave a jerky nod. "Sure was, Mr. Peat. From down at Pine Ridge."

"I used to know some kinfolks of yours," he said. "Real interestin' fellow...." He added up her groceries and wrote down the total in Mrs. Bragg's book.

But when Hemmy Wiggins was again sputtering up the road, he tore out the sheet and left money for her entire account in the cash box. Any relative of Bud Hinkle, he felt, was a friend of his.

Writing for children is great fun, particularly since I never quite gave up being a child myself.

THE JEWELED MOUSE

There was nothing in all the civilized world like the closet of Princess Clorinda. Besides chests filled with satins and velvets and cloth-of-gold dresses, it contained the most wonderful toys ever dreamed of.

There were dolls whose eyes were made of real sapphires and whose hair was spun of gold. There were dolls with emerald eyes and carved jade hair. There was a rocking horse of ebony with ruby nostrils and onyx eyes. There were so many wonders there that it would take an entire book to describe them all, and even then one might easily overlook the two most wonderful things of all.

On a shelf in the corner sat a topaz cat. When you stroked it on the head, it would purr in a rather mechanical way. When you pulled its tail, it pursued a jeweled mouse all around the room, growling ferociously.

The mouse itself was beautiful, as well as very, very fast on its small velvet feet. When the cat began to move, the mouse's tail (a rope of pearls), would stiffen, and the creature would search frantically for a mouse-hole. Unfortunately, as it was an artificial mouse, it always chose things that looked like holes...shadows and dark spots on the carpet.

The cat always caught it, though as it had no real teeth no harm was done to the mouse.

These were gifts to Clorinda from her Aunt Athelia, who was a wizardess. On a recent visit, Athelia had held her niece on her knee and looked into her eyes. There she saw a shadow that troubled her greatly, and she laid two fingers lightly on Clorinda's head and listened to her heart. That told her the reason for the child's sadness, though only a wizardess could have understood what she heard.

Clorinda was lonely. Though she had the most loving of parents, and they all lived in a small but tasteful castle with green fields and lush orchards all about it, she had no playmates. Not one.

Of course, she often went into the orchards to talk with the gardeners or into the hen-runs and the pigsties behind the castle stables to talk with the servants. Yet they were busy and had no time to talk with little girls, even a princess.

Even those marvelous things in the closet did not make her happy, for there was no one to share them. Her croquet lawn, her tennis court, the bowling green on the lawn, were no good to her alone. She had no sister or brother, and not one of the noble families nearby had a child near her age. Theirs were all grown up or else were tiny infants.

Of course, the people who served the castle and the noble houses had children. The village fairly swarmed with them, but their parents never thought to lend one of their small Robs or Sallys to their adored princess. Who would have thought she might be lonely?

Athelia, being a wizardess, saw, of course, and she was patient, for an impatient magician can get into all sorts of terrible jams. She sent her niece the topaz cat, which was only what it seemed, and the jeweled mouse, which held some of her very best magic.

However, Clorinda seldom went into her closet, except to choose her gown for the day. It made her lonelier than ever to look at those toys, for she had nobody to help her play with them. The mouse sat on the shelf, unpursued by the cat, for a year and three days.

It had begun to think, in its magical-mechanical mind, that it might never have a chance to do the things Athelia had created it to accomplish. And then came Wanda, the very young chambermaid, to dust the closet and to check the toys for moth or rust.

Did I mention the stuffed toys? No? Then I must do so at once. They were incredibly lifelike, being real animals that the King's forester had killed in the hunt. The King's tanner had skinned them, sending the meat to the kitchens and treating the skins to make them quite natural. Then the Queen's seamstresses had sewed them back together and stuffed them with soft materials. The jeweler had fitted them with the most lifelike of gemmed eyes and the most elaborate of collars. They did, however, tend to get moth in their fur.

Clorinda hated them, though she was too polite to say so. When guests came and asked to see them, she brought them out, though she really disliked touching them, as they were so stiff and lifeless.

Wanda was checking the stuffed animals for moth, drawing nearer and nearer the corner where the mouse had been waiting for a year and three days. Ruby eyes twinkling, he watched her approach, as he gathered his watch-spring muscles in anticipation.

When Wanda came into range, he scooted forward before she could notice him and plunked into her apron pocket. He was so small that the added weight wasn't noticeable, though she turned to stare at the spot where she had seen something move.

"Was that a mouse?" she asked Clorinda, who was busy bouncing a gilded leather ball in the doorway. The ball didn't bounce at all well, but rubber had not yet been discovered, and it was the best to be had.

"I didn't see a thing," said Clorinda. But if she had looked closely, she might have missed the glint of the mouse's pearl-rimmed ruby eyes in the dark corner where he stayed.

The jeweled mouse was on his way, and in some ways this first step was the hardest. He felt a bit frightened at leaving the safety of the shelf, and he wondered if he could possibly do the thing Athelia had directed him to do.

But things moved quickly; if he had been prone to dizziness, the magical-mechanical mouse might have become giddy. Wanda went back to the kitchen, whisking down the long corridors and down the flights of marble stairs, and took off her dusting apron. She donned a grubby one in which to peel potatoes for her aunt, the cook, and hung the fancy apron on a peg in the closet, along with mops and brooms and feather-dusters.

When Ben, the under-forester, came to get his lunch, he went into the closet to put away his jacket, and as he passed the apron the mouse gave a desperate leap. He went, head-first, into the man's game bag, which he carried on his shoulder. He felt a twitch, but he thought he had caught the strap on a peg and paid it no heed.

It didn't take Ben long to eat, for he had a pile of timber to cut and stack. The King, unlike some, provided free fuel for his people in winter, and the foresters worked at cutting it all the summer. They kept the forest tidy and got the woodcutting done, all with the same effort. When Ben went back to work, the mouse went with him.

No matter how magical or mechanical a mouse may be, and no matter how good its intentions, it can still find it very hard to pick the right sort of playmate for a real live princess. The jeweled mouse had never seen a child other than Clorinda, and as it rode in the game bag it tried to think what sort of creature might work best.

When the forester set his bag beneath a tree and took up his axe again, the mouse peered out and stared around. He had never dreamed of a place filled with large trees, and at first it seemed there was nobody there to approach at all. But in time he saw a pair of bright eyes staring from a hole beneath a bush. He scampered out of the bag and hurried over to the dark space.

Ordinarily, mice and badgers do not speak the same language, but Athelia had thought of everything, and the mouse understood the big creature perfectly. He was able to coax the beast from its hole, and when it came out, he was mightily impressed with its striped fur coat. It had strong bowed legs and a rather fierce expression, but he thought it might do very well.

"Would you like to live in the castle and play with the princess?" he asked it at once.

The badger looked puzzled for a moment, and its forehead wrinkled with thought. "Might's well give ut a try," it said at last.

"Then take me up in your teeth and carry me back. I will show you the way," said the mouse.

That was easy enough, but when Cook opened the kitchen door to throw out a pan of water, she saw the striped animal and began to shriek. Wanda came to her aid, and then pots and skillets and griddles began to fly, as the two flung anything that came to hand.

No sane badger would remain in such a place, and he dropped the mouse into a rosebush and fled for his life. The mouse was very still until the women calmed down. Then he crept out and brushed the thorns from his jeweled back.

He felt discouraged, but he was not one to give up without a struggle. Back to work he went.

There was a potato basket against the wall beside the rosebush. He hid in that while considering what to do next, burrowing beneath a sack laid in its bottom. Before he had calmed down, the basket was lifted and taken away. All the mouse could do was hide, and hope that he was going someplace where there might be a playmate for Clorinda.

The basket swung dizzily and sat down with a thump. A big voice called, "Fill this 'un and I'll take t'other to the potato house."

The mouse risked scrabbling up the side of the basket to peep over the edge. There was a potato field, with row after row of plants that had been plowed up and waited for the farmers to pick up the potatoes growing at their roots. Men and women were bent over the soil, grubbing out the potatoes and shaking the earth from them. Even as he watched, a rain of potatoes was flung at the basket where he hid.

With a tiny shriek, he fled into the rows of plants and

scuttered blindly until he came to a stone fence. He climbed up to rest and clean the potato dust off himself. He found a chink just the right size for him among the climbing honeysuckle vines, which bloomed in a thick mass that almost covered the stones. Daisies smiled up from the green turf below. It was a lovely place, almost nicer than Clorinda's closet.

The sun shone, and two butterflies swooped about, landing first on one blossom and then on another. The mouse thought of asking one of those to go with him, but they looked too fragile to last for long.

He sat in his sunny niche, thinking and thinking. He knew he must move soon, but the sun was so warm, and his watch spring muscles were so tired, that he began to doze.

A quiet brown head rose amid the daisies, followed by a sleek and slithery body. A forked tongue licked out as if checking how a mouse might taste. Something about that flat black gaze roused the mouse at once.

Even as the snake struck, he squeaked and leaped, making it to the top of the wall faster than any real mouse could have done. He ran along the rough stones, scrabbling and dislodging gravels, startling sparrows and hedgebirds that preened there in the sunlight.

When he could run no more, he paused in a shadow and tried to think what to do. It looked hopeless. And what might Athelia do to a mouse that failed? A magical-mechanical mouse who did not find a playmate for her niece? He shuddered at the thought. At the very least, she might remove his jewels and set them into rings.

As he mused, a hand reached down and lifted him. "Now what a pretty thing!" said a bumbling voice. "Here on the fence, left alone and abandoned. Might be, t'will comfort young Cricket, and her alone and crying for her sick mother. She shall have a look at it, no matter if some'un comes looking for it later. Just the thing!" The hand thrust the mouse into a ragged pocket, and he rocked there as long legs strode and the voice still bumbled to itself.

At last they paused. The hand burrowed down to the bottom of the pocket, where the mouse cowered among keys and old nails and a pocket knife and a grimy kerchief. It fumbled a bit, found him, and pulled him into the light.

"Now, Cricket-me-dear, come to see what your old friend has brought," called the voice. "I found it atop the wall, yonder, all bright and beautiful. It might belong to the Princess herself, so fine it is."

The mouse could see now over the top of a low stone wall into a tiny garden, aflame with moss-roses and pinks and hollyhocks. A tiny house sat in its middle. On the doorstep sat a little girl in a torn yellow frock.

Her face was buried in her lap, but the sound of the voice brought her up to stare at the browned old man holding the mouse. She wiped her eyes on a corner of her apron and came to join him.

"Good day, Grandsir Fred. What have you found?" There was still a trace in her voice of the hiccups that crying always causes, but she was quite polite and under control.

"Why this. 'Tis not much to take the place of your dear Mama, but mayhap it will keep you company until she is better and can come home."

Cricket saw the mouse just as he saw her clearly. Each said silently, inside themselves, "The very thing!" He rushed into her hands as quickly as they came to him, and she stood clasping him, turning him over and over.

"Oh, the pretty stones in his back! And see...his eyes have white beads around them. And his tail...his cunning little pearl tail!"

The old fellow was chuckling at the success of his find. Cricket hugged him well and thanked him, and he kissed her on the forehead and touched the mouse with a cautious finger.

"It may be, Cricket, that someone at t' castle lost this. I cannot give it ye as a gift, for it may belong to someone else, but if it cheers you a wee bit, then I am content. And the word is that your Mama is much better, and the Sisters of the Sick will send her home before long."

Cricket smiled. "I see, Grandsir Fred. Do you think I should take this to the castle and see if anyone has lost it? Then I will know for certain."

The mouse almost jumped from her hand in his excitement. It had been wondering how it might force such a large and self-willed thing as a human child to do what he wanted, and here she was volunteering to go.

"A good notion," said Fred, as he ambled away along the path.

Before he was out of sight, Cricket went into the house and put on her best gown and her straw hat. Then she set out, mouse in hand, for the castle.

Now the mouse rode high and free, seeing the road and the houses along it, as well as the fields in the distance. They passed the stone wall, too, and he marveled that he had managed to cover so great a distance.

When Cricket started to turn in at the kitchen gate of the castle, the mouse wriggled hard in her hand. She looked down, startled.

"No! No!" shrieked the mouse, using human language for the first time in his life. "Go to the front gate! Ask for the Princess! Come, child, don't gape! Go nicely, there's a good child, and do as I say!"

Cricket was reared to be obedient, and she did as he said, though never before had she had to obey a jeweled mouse. However when she asked the tall guard in the busby hat for the Princess Clorinda, he showed her in quite as if she were expected and welcome.

The First Footman showed her to the second floor, where the Second Footman took over, guiding her to the door of the tower where Clorinda had her rooms. Wanda met them there.

"And what might you want with the Princess, Child?" she asked.

"I wondered...has she lost this?" quavered Cricket, holding up the jeweled mouse.

Wanda's mouth dropped open. Before she said a word, the mouse said, "Indeed, Wanda, you know she did. Now be a good girl and take us to Clorinda's playroom. I know that she's probably sitting at the window with a book in her lap and her thoughts far away. Why are you gaping at me? Come, come, Wanda! My word!"

The mouse, you will note, was getting carried away with being able to order large humans about. But Wanda did as she was told, not being quite able to find words to argue with a mouse.

When she led Cricket into the playroom, Clorinda looked up with her usual daydreamy expression...only to see another little girl and begin to look happier by the minute. Wanda was very glad she had not argued.

"Oh, stay and play with me," Clorinda begged Cricket.

"I can stay until Mama comes home from the house of healing," said Cricket. "I am all alone at home."

"Then you shall stay with me until she is better, and we will play together every day. Come and see all my toys in the closet!"

Somehow, it was a totally different closet, with another child there to marvel at the dolls and the other toys. Even the stuffed animals seemed livelier than ever before.

Soon the playroom was awash with toys. The topaz cat, taken down from its shelf, dashed after the jeweled mouse, but it no longer was able to catch him. Having some experience of the world, now, the mouse no longer was deceived by shadows or dark spots and hid in real nooks.

The cat, frustrated, ran in circles, spitting topaz curses. Wanda swept them up, later, and strung them into a necklace for her aunt, the Cook, to wear to church.

When Clorinda's parents found that Cricket's mother would never be able to work in the fields again, they moved her, with Cricket, into the castle, where she learned needlework. You can imagine that this suited both children very well.

They had spats, from time to time, but that only kept their friendship from growing dull. They studied together and played together and became the very best of friends.

The toy closet was busy. The dolls lost their look of newness and began to look well-loved. The stuffed animals began to show wear, and the topaz cat used up all its topaz curses. The rocking horse wore down its rockers until it positively seemed to buck.

But the jeweled mouse...ah, he only got better and

brighter and wiser and quieter. For he was, after all, a magical-mechanical mouse, and that is the very best kind.

This began as a single story, "The Very Strange War," published in Trailblazer *back in 1973, but other stories came, so I kept adding them until they formed an overall story.*

THE KINGDOM OF YIP

BEING A TALE OF KINGS AND ANIMALS AND PRINCES—AND, OF COURSE, WOLVES

PART ONE

THE VERY STRANGE WAR

There was once a small and peaceful kingdom called Yip. It lay on the border between I-Wish-It-Would and I-Wonder-When, and it was ruled by a brave but foolish king called Yubert. The only sensible thing he ever did was to marry a merry lady and help her to bring up their son, Robilot.

Robilot was just what a prince should be. He was brave, but prudent. He was truthful, but kind. He was very wise, indeed, for his age. Unfortunately, when he was only ten years old, his father bravely (and foolishly) spurred his horse toward a high fence. The horse, being wiser than Yubert, stopped short, but the king kept going over the fence. So Robilot was king.

When the people had finished wiping away their tears (for Yubert, however foolish, was kind and good), they began to cheer for Robilot. This made him feel rather strange inside, and he thought, *If they are going to cheer for me, I must deserve their cheers and be worthy of their trust.*

So he decided to ride around the countryside, talking with the people and finding out their problems and needs. This was very easy to do, for nobody pays much attention to a little boy.

Luckily, the kingdom of Yip had not yet invented photography, so nobody knew what the new king looked like. His state portraits were very grand and stiff, so that when Robilot had a little dirt on his nose and was wearing a ragged tunic, he didn't look like the portrait at all.

His plan might have worked, except for one thing. People who are busily plowing and planting and spinning and sweeping and cobbling and tailoring and making milk jugs cannot be bothered to stop and tell their troubles to a ten-year-old boy. So Robilot wandered about, watching the people work.

He learned a great deal about plowing and cobbling and making milk jugs, but he learned more about the people. Although they were mostly honest and thrifty and hard-working, he found they were afraid of a great many things.

They were afraid of being laughed at; they were afraid

of losing their familiar ways of life. They were terribly afraid of getting hurt or of being uncomfortable. And Robilot wondered, *What would I do if I ever needed an army to defend our country?*

He asked several persons whom he met on the road, "What would you do if there were a war?"

And they always replied, "Oh! I would run away into the mountains with my family and my money and only come back when there was peace."

After a while, he stopped asking people about things. Instead he thought, *My father's horse was quite a bit wiser, in his way, than my father. I wonder if the bee-keeper's bees and the herder's cows and the swineherd's pigs are a little wiser than their masters?*

So he began going among the animals in the farms he passed. He talked to them stirringly about their country. He appealed to their good sense and to their patriotism. Of course, they couldn't answer him, but they seemed to be considering what he said. Many of them nodded wisely and winked one eye as he spoke.

His mother had allowed him one month to go about the kingdom. After that, she said, people would begin to wonder where he was and what he was doing, and she could not put them off forever. A month later, he stole into the kitchen hallway, late one evening, and became a king again.

The very next day, the Prime Minister sent for him in great haste and met him at the door of the State Chamber.

"Your Majesty," he quavered, trembling with agitation, "I have terrible news. My spies in I-Wonder-When report that King Grapnel the Fifth called in his War Minister last night and asked him this: 'I wonder when someone is going to invade Yip? It should be very easy, because the ruler is only a boy. Yubert was too brave to bother, but a child should be simple to overthrow.'"

"Do we have an army?" asked Robilot.

"There used to be about twenty men in the Royal Guard." The Prime Minister sounded doubtful.

"Is that all?"

"Most of the policemen in Yip City would probably volunteer," whispered the Prime Minister.

"Write a proclamation." commanded Robilot. "Tell the people that we must fight, for my father always told me King Grapnel is both wicked and greedy. He would tax us to starvation, and he would let his soldiers pasture their horses in the fields and gardens, so we would go hungry in the winter."

So the proclamation was written.

But nobody volunteered. Not even the police. When the scout rode in, shouting that the army of the invaders had crossed the border, many of the Yipians headed for the mountains, and the rest locked themselves in their houses and hid under beds and in closets.

Robilot took his father's sword, which tripped him repeatedly, and the smallest helmet he could find. He sent his mother to saddle his pony, because all the servants had hidden or fled. Not even the Prime Minister could be found.

Robilot rode away all alone, his helmet banging his nose, a shield flopping against his knee, and his sword held straight up, to keep it from tripping the pony.

Now one might think that cows and horses and pigs and sheep and bees and poultry would never be interested in politics. One would be quite right, too. But they heard the proclamation, for loud-voiced heralds had shouted it up and down all the roads in the kingdom and at every town square.

The animals felt, quite sensibly, that if the people grew hungry, the first to feel the results would be themselves. Besides, when they saw the tired little pony trotting down the dusty road with his lonely rider trying to find a way to blow his nose with his head in a helmet, they remembered the boy who had talked with them about the kingdom.

* * * * * * *

When King Grapnel, looking splendid in crimson velvet over silver armor, halted on top of the first hill in Yip, he looked over a broad valley, rich with ripening grain. He smiled a greedy smile, as his gaze followed the road toward Yip City, where a cloud of dust was slowly coming toward him.

"We shall wait here." he told his generals. "They will be forced to attack uphill. We'll wipe whatever army they have completely off the map."

But as the army drew nearer, the king's expression changed. Coming up the hill was a very strange group, led by a child on a dust-coated pony. There were cattle and goats, sheep and pigs, geese hissing like tea-kettles, chickens squawking, bulls bellowing. Yet all of them were moving together.

"Let's scatter this rabble!" shouted Grapnel, white with rage. But when the horses charged down the hill, the pigs ran between their hooves, bringing down horses and riders in a dreadful tumble of armor and whinnies and waving legs.

The geese rushed in, tweaking off helmets and pinching noses. The other fowl followed, squawking and bravely pecking whatever they could reach with their sharp beaks.

The bulls stood firm against the rest of the horsemen, shaking their great heads, snorting through red nostrils, and flashing their sharp horns until the horses (who disapproved of battle) grew nervous and unmanageable.

The sheep, baaing and trampling, went over what was down, under what was up, between what was separated. They made so much dust and noise it was impossible for an order to be heard. Many a fallen rider, tweaked by geese and pecked by hens, found himself staring up into the untidy nose and silly eyes of one of these unlikely warriors, turned over, and wept into the dust.

Then came the bees. At first, Grapnel thought a storm was approaching, and he shouted like a madman, "Get up, you idiots! Get up, you cowards! These cattle will flee the storm!"

Slowly the riders remounted and grouped together in a huddle, surrounded by all the glowering beasts. And then the bees came down in a zinging, stinging cloud. The sturdy war-horses had enough. They broke from formation, leaped sheep and geese, and set out for home at top speed. Their riders didn't discourage them. King Grapnel, stung and swollen, turned his back upon the ripe fields of Yip and cursed along in the rear.

Robilot, tired and hot and dusty, with his nose still unblown, sat and watched him go. Then he took off his helmet, blew his nose long and hard, and said to the animals milling about him, "Yip is going to have a flag. It will be green, like the fields, and on it will be a cow, a goat, a sheep, and a pig, with poultry around their feet. There will be bees all around the edge."

That is just what happened. And King Grapnel did not dare attack again for a long, long while.

PART TWO

THE SHEPHERD OF YIP

Rolph, son of Rulf, son of Ralph, stood by the door of his mother's cottage and gazed westward, toward the mountains which separated the land of Yip from its neighbor, I-Wish-It-Would. His heart was as heavy as the pack that he must soon lift to his shoulder. Tears hung just behind the edges of his eyes and he blinked hard, so that his mother would not notice them, when she came to bid him goodbye.

In the roadway before the hut, a hundred sheep milled and bleated, waiting for him to take them high into those mountains for their summer of grazing and growing fat. Two sheep-dogs, nervous and alert, moved back and forth between the flock and Rolph, knowing that soon they would be off on their yearly journey with this new master.

Rolph's mother came to the door of their home with a last parcel to tuck into his pack. She smoothed his rough brown hair as she leaned to kiss him; then she said, "My son, I know that your father would be proud of you, if he were here. Men of our family have always tended the sheep for the people of Yip. No other family has ever been entrusted with them. Some doubted, last winter, that your father was wise in giving the responsibility to you, and you only eleven.

"But, as he lay dying, he said to me, 'Rolph has been at my side every summer since he was six. He knows the sheep; he knows the mountains. Being the grandson of my father, he is no coward. And he has a good head. If he were forty, he would be no better shepherd than he is now. Tell him, as he goes upon his journey, that he is a true son of the house of Ralph, and that I love him.'"

Rolph lifted his head and smiled at his mother. Not a tear escaped to spoil his farewell. "Look for me when the leaves turn, Mother. The sheep and I will be home safely by then, never fear."

With a whistle to the dogs, he took up his pack and fastened the straps about his shoulders. Then, staff in hand, he trudged away toward the mountains, a lonely figure amid the dust stirred by the sheep.

A glow of pride warmed his heart when he thought of his father's words, but, deep within him, he knew that he would never have chosen to be a shepherd. The thought of the lonely summer ahead filled him with gloom.

"How I would love to go to Yip City," he said to himself. "And perhaps find work to do for King Robilot. How fine it would be to ride down the way on a great horse, waving a banner and crying 'Way for the King! Way for the King!'"

His eyes glowed as he pictured the figure he would cut, the people scurrying out of the way, the royal carriage rattling along behind him.

And then a wayward ewe fell into the ditch and lay there, bleating fretfully, until he hauled her out.

* * * * * * *

Far to the west, Old Grizzle, the wolf, followed by his hungry family, limped across the stony hills toward the mountains of Yip. For many years, they had picked a scant living from the scraggly herds owned by the people of I-Wish-It-Would, and he was getting old, dreaming of fatter herds browsing on greener pastures.

So he set his eyes upon the grassy heights of Yip and lolloped along, his red tongue hanging down between his white teeth. In a day and a night, Grizzle's pack had reached the rocky crags above the pasture-lands.

In the evening of the day after that, Rolph and his charges arrived, too. The woolly flock trampled and baaed in their silly sheep way as Rolph urged them up the narrow path. Far and Near, as the two dogs were called, nipped at flanks and barked at noses, when the animals tried to turn back, and Rolph waved his staff and smacked any laggards. Then Caesar, the great ram, smelled the fresh grass and pure water waiting ahead. Up the path he went, and the herd rolled smoothly after him.

* * * * * * *

Old Grizzle, lazing on a sun-warmed rock high above, heard the din and smelled the rank sheep smell long before the herd came into view. He flattened himself upon the ledge and grinned a wide red grin of joy.

* * * * * * *

Below, Rolph put away his pack in the stone hut his

grandfather's father had built, lit a small fire on the blackened rock hearth, and cooked his meal cakes for supper. Far and Near stood at the door, wagging their tails and gazing hungrily at the cakes.

A whisper of breeze stirred across the meadow, curled about the crag, and drifted past the hut. Far and Near stiffened. Their neck-hair bristling, they gazed up at the crag and growled deep in their throats. Rolph looked up and said, "Check the sheep, boys."

Like twin bullets, the two sped down the meadow, rounded the far side of the flock, and came panting back to the hut. Though they had found nothing amiss, they still growled gruffly, their ears twitching at every sound.

Rolph stood in the doorway, looking up, as the dogs had. Several times, he had seen his father battle wolves, sometimes with great fires, sometimes fighting them off with his staff, while a smaller Rolph flung stones. But it was eerie and lonely to feel the presence of an enemy when he was alone.

Rolph's eyes grew heavy, as the moon rolled over the misty ridge of mountains, but he did not unroll his blankets inside the hut. Instead, he made his bed at the higher end of the valley, so that any creature that made its way down from the heights would have to pass close by. The dog Far curled up against a rock on the other side of the herd, while Near remained close to Rolph. All slept, but with one ear tuned to the night-sounds about them.

* * * * * * *

Grizzle looked down at the quiet flock, the drowsy watchers. But he was old and canny. He never hurried, and he never leaped without knowing where he would fall. So he found a comfortable place near his mate, turned around three times, curled up with his nose covered by the brush of his tail, and went soundly to sleep.

* * * * * * *

When the sun rose, it found Rolph already awake, ready to drive the sheep to higher pastures. Far and Near raced about the meadow, playing with their shadows, leaping after butterflies, shaking the sleep out of their bones. But at Rolph's whistle they came to attention, taking their places and beginning to drive the herd up the slope.

As Rolph climbed after, he felt the chilly shiver between his shoulders that told him he was being watched.

Caesar, the ram, also felt those watching eyes, as he moved along. Somewhere in his dim sheep mind there was a memory of wolves.

Well before noon, Rolph had his charges grazing on the mountainside, while he, with Far and Near at his side, sat in the shadow of a boulder and watched. The day crept by very slowly, and the boy felt his loneliness more and more. The summer seemed to stretch out before him in an endless chain of long days. He thought of his father, who had always been with him, teaching him the lore of the mountain herbs, the ways of the birds and animals, and tales of the old times when their ancestors had been faced with danger to their flocks.

"Even when Father was here, I was lonely," he said to Far, scratching him under the side of the chin, while the dog whined with pleasure. "Oh, I wish...I wish my family had been shoemakers or bakers. I wish I could live near people and do important work in the world. Who knows or cares if a boy named Rolph is awake or asleep on the mountain?"

But he did not sleep. And when the sun began to disappear toward I-Wish-It-Would, he whistled to the dogs and took up his staff. The herd moved slowly down the steep way, thirsty for the water that lay below, but so stuffed with grass that there was no hurrying them. And as they went, clouds began to drift across the mountaintops and mist followed them along the trail, so that when they reached the meadow Rolph could hardly see from one edge of the flock to the other as he counted his charges.

He ate his supper hurriedly. Then he went out into the open and built a large fire, using the stock of wood which his father had gathered the summer before. His back against a rock, his staff across his knees, he set himself to wait and watch all the night long. Far and Near paced nervously about the edges of the flock, pausing, now and then, to push their chilly noses into Rolph's hand.

* * * * * * *

Old Grizzle and his pack were no longer on the ledge. Covered by the blanket of mist, they had crept down to the meadow. Tonight, Grizzle felt in his bones, he would have a taste of fat lamb again. He watched the flicker of the fire warily, biding his time.

* * * * * * *

The fog grew thicker; the fire burned low. Rolph nodded between the two dogs.

* * * * * * *

Grizzle grinned, slipping down the slope toward the flock and a fat lamb that dozed beside its mother. With a lunge and a snap, he caught the little animal, but he missed the throat, and it began bleating, while the other sheep milled madly, worried by the rest of the wolves.

Caesar, dreaming uneasily nearby, heaved to his feet. He remembered that smell! Wolf! Pushing the frantic ewes aside, he pounded toward the commotion.

Rolph and the dogs were speeding across the meadow the instant they heard the lamb's cry. A dreadful bleating tumble of sheep showed where the wolves snarled and slashed away at the flock.

The heavy staff whirled about the boy's head, as he drove into the midst of the struggle, with Far and Near beside him. Ears flattened, eyes glinting angrily, the dogs flung themselves at the beasts, taking two of the young wolves out of the fight. Rolph charged at Grizzle, cracking him on the nose and the forelegs with his staff.

Stunned, Grizzle rolled away, and his mate turned from the sheep, her eyes shining green and deadly as she leaped at the boy. Another young wolf caught him by the leg, and Rolph went down beneath a gray and furry tangle.

And now Caesar sprang from the herd, his head, with its flat curly horns, held low like a true "battering ram." He hit Grizzle's mate fairly in the side and the breath went out of her in a surprised "whuff!"

This freed Rolph's hands again, and he caught up a stone and beat the young wolf from his torn ankle. Catching up his staff, he faced Grizzle again, and with a great cry he began beating the beast until its skull rang.

With a howl, the wolf gave up the fight, tucked his tail, and fled for the high crags. After him sped his mate and his young, hotly pursued by Rolph, the two dogs, and the enraged Caesar, who, blind with anger, butted anything that got in his way.

Far over the mountains the wolf family ran, back into the safe, scanty pastures of I-Wish-It-Would, where no one bothered about a missing lamb or cared to pursue a wolfish thief.

Limping, breathless and sore, Rolph and his comrades went down into the meadow, through the ragged mists, to the comfort of the fire. From his pack, Rolph took ointment and bandages. Far and Near sat patiently as he bound up bitten paws and torn ears and rubbed the salve into the cuts in their necks. Then he cleaned and bandaged his ankle and leg.

"You were my brave boys!" he said to the dogs. "Father would be proud of you. We gave them a fight they'll never forget. We...why I guess we fought a real war, just the four of us. The sheep are safe for now, though we'll have to watch even sharper.

"I suppose we are doing important work for the King. And maybe it doesn't make any difference whether anyone knows what we've done. We know, and I have a feeling that Father knows, too. He and Grandfather, and all the men of our family who have fought wolves on this very mountain."

He stretched out before the fire, with Far's head on his stomach and Near's head on his feet. He yawned and his eyes began to close.

"Perhaps," he said sleepily, "There are much worse

things than to be a shepherd of Yip."

And he went peacefully to sleep.

PART THREE

THE GRASP OF GRAPNEL

King Grapnel squirmed uncomfortably upon his throne. His chin was propped peevishly on his hand. His brows were wrinkled furiously over his small eyes. His face wore his plotting-and-scheming expression.

His Prime Minister fidgeted nearby, standing first upon one foot, then the other, cracking his knuckles and scratching his long thin nose. Now and again, he would look sideways at the King, wondering if the result of all this plotting-and scheming would be as uncomfortable for the country as other results had been before. Often, he would sigh and stare at his boots, wishing that he had taken up tailoring or baking, instead of Prime-Ministering.

"Our national pride has been flung into the dirt!" the King suddenly shouted. "Those nip-noses of Yip humiliated our cavalry past endurance. The idea of sending a gaggle of geese and a parcel of piglets against the assembled power of I-Wonder-When leaves one gasping with its gall. The insult has rankled within us for a year. Our rage increases every hour. This injury must be washed out—in blood!"

The Prime Minister blanched. This was even worse than he had supposed in his gloomiest supposings.

"Er, Your Majesty, I hope you are not thinking of returning to your campaign against Yip," he faltered. "You know, when such a thing is mentioned, all the cavalry officers go to bed with stomach-aches, and such an uproar arises among the troops that they must be given long leaves of absence to quiet their nerves. Even the horses fling off their saddles and run into the forest."

"Do you take me for a fool, Sir?" roared the King. "Not toward Yip do I turn my eyes...yet. We must rebuild the confidence of our armies. We need an EASY victory. We need to feel the crunch of fallen enemies beneath the hooves of our mounts. We need to smell the smoke of burning villages and to taste the sweetness of stolen meats. We need to be a conquering army, once again."

The Prime Minister sighed with relief. "Whom do you have in mind?" he asked. "To conquer, I mean."

"I had thought," drawled the King, with an evil grin, "Of the lazy little kingdom of I-Wish-It-Would. No," he said, as the Prime Minister looked alarmed. "We'd not try to go across Yip to get there. We will go along the River Olo, keeping strictly to our own side, and we shall cross the shallows well past the northern tip of Yip. Then it should be simple to rampage down through the sheep pastures to come upon the capital city, before anyone knows we are there." He grinned again, so grimly that even the Prime Minister felt a cold shiver trickle down his back.

"It sounds like a very good plan, Your Majesty. Surely, there could be no danger in attacking so disorganized a country as I-Wish-It-Would. The plan should be practical, very practical, indeed," said the Prime Minister, happy to find that the plot was no worse.

And so the orders were issued. The cavalry officers got out of bed and polished up their swords. The troopers came back from their long leaves, and the cavalry combed the forests until all the horses were caught.

Supplies were loaded onto carts. All the people were given strictest orders to stand beside the road and cheer for the troops as they rode away. Everyone seemed well content with the prospect of looting the towns and villages of I-Wish-It-Would.

Everyone except the horses. Well they remembered their last military experience. The hiss of geese and the bellowing of bulls still rang in their ears. The buzzing of the most casual of bees still left them shaking. Never particularly fond of the business of battle, they had, in the invasion of Yip, found a situation that made them positively hate the thought of war. So they trotted out of the capital city of Soon with their heads high but their hearts filled with dread.

The long line of cavalry and spearmen and carts wound down from the hills around the city of Soon, until they reached the dusty track that followed the River Olo. Long coils of dust rose behind the army, as they trampled through stickery thickets and gnat-infested marshes.

King Grapnel, riding just behind the scouts, glowered sternly ahead, but his great charger, Nemesis, glanced nervously after every sound and twitched his delicate ears at every insect buzz. And all along the army's line of march, the horses shied and snorted and shivered their skins.

The men of Yip, fishing along the river, saw the ominous trail of dust hanging upon the air, and they left their nets and set out in haste for the nearest outpost of King Robilot's new Yipian army. The people of Yip remembered with shame how their country had been saved by their ten-year-old ruler and his improbable collection of animals and poultry and bees. So they had rallied to the service of their country until a fine army had been trained to defend them against any invader. Even those who were not in the army were eager to serve their king.

Quickly the news sped to Yip City, carried by couriers on swift horses, and before nightfall the king had set spies to track the forces of King Grapnel, reporting each hour upon his direction and his probable goal.

Then Robilot sent specially instructed messengers to carry the news to Someday, the capitol of I-Wish-It-Would, for when King Grapnel moved his troops, all his neighbors watched with apprehension.

Far to the west, in the sheep pastures of I-Wish-It-Would, the angry, hungry family of Old Grizzle, the wolf, raged across the countryside, sore of hide and of temper, ready to pick a fight with anyone. Driven from the mountains of Yip by Rolph, the shepherd, they snarled and slavered up and down the parched pastures, looking for trouble.

Watched by hidden eyes, King Grapnel urged his followers on, setting a pace that irritated the horses and wearied the men. When a cart axle broke, the King fumed and fizzed like a Roman candle. When a string of pack-horses broke free and ran away into a marsh, he turned a dangerous color and muttered under his helmet.

His Prime Minister, miserable in his armor, tried in vain to calm his angry ruler, but Grapnel was beyond reason. His only thought was of battle and sudden death; his only desire was to harden his men until they could again face the unorthodox forces of Yip.

When they reached the shallow rapids of the River

Olo, beyond the northern border of Yip, the army of I-Wonder-When was dusty and hungry and weary. Even the King could see that he could drive them no farther that day.

"Tomorrow," he told the Prime Minister, "We shall cross into I-Wish-It-Would, and by noon I shall sit in the prince's palace, dictating the terms of surrender to Prince Blunder."

"I devoutly hope so," said the Prime Minister, removing his helmet and wiping the gnats from his eyebrows with a silk handkerchief. "Let us hope, Your Majesty, that no one has noticed that you are moving the army. A surprise attack is so much more successful when it is...er...a surprise, you know."

The King gave a snort of utter scorn and stalked into his tent, leaving the poor Prime Minister to find the softest spot he could and spread his blanket. After grubbing out several roots and rocks and unidentified knots, the poor man settled down for the night, secretly wishing that King Grapnel were at the bottom of some particularly deep sea.

The sun rose, next morning, upon a scene of confusion. Sleepy officers yawned orders to half-awake troopers. Breakfast made things no better, as what wasn't scorched was cold. The horses preferred freedom to saddles and packs and kicked up many a struggle, with the hostlers and the troopers shouting and swearing. Only the King was armed and alert and ready to move on.

With an uproar of splashing and snorting, the army waded into the shallows at last, and made for the opposite shore, which marked the boundary of the principality of I-Wish-It-Would. Before long, the entire force had crossed over and was standing, dripping and cross, waiting for

King Grapnel's commands.

The shepherds of I-Wish-It-Would were a slack-twisted lot and seldom were up and about before the sun was high. Their lean flocks would stand, baaing and milling in the dust, waiting for their lazy masters to drive them to better pastures, while the overworked sheep-dogs circled and watched, keeping their charges from running away into the mountains.

On this morning, the shepherds were due for a dreadful surprise, for, just as they were about to begin moving their flocks, a large army appeared over the horizon, trotting steadily toward the south, where the capital city lay. As they drew near, squads of troopers dropped aside and rounded up all the sheep, driving them away behind the invading army.

The swiftest of the shepherds was sent to carry the news, traveling secret paths and old shortcuts so that he could reach the nearest village before the invaders could surprise its inhabitants. He arrived too late and found only blazing houses and ruined fields where the village had stood. The villagers came out of hiding and stood with him, weeping for their lost homes and shaking their fists after the disappearing army.

King Grapnel now rode in the very forefront of the army, gazing grimly ahead, tasting already the fruits of his victory. So intent was he upon his thoughts that he never noticed that Nemesis was growing more and more nervous, whiffling through widened nostrils and cocking his ears this way and that.

The troopers were having trouble with their horses. The drivers of the carts were growing very hot and red-faced, and their language was getting worse by the minute, as the cart-horses danced sideways in the traces or stopped still and whinnied.

There was good reason for their nervousness. Just over the next hillock, Old Grizzle and his sons and dozens of wolves they had routed out of the mountains and plains were gathered, ready to make a raid on the sheep pastures. All were lean and hungry and angry and ready for trouble in any form.

So King Grapnel, locked in his daydream, found himself in the midst of a pack of red-eyed wolves that leaped for his horse's throat and nipped at his own royal heels.

A dreadful turmoil arose, as the cavalry horses reared and stamped and snorted. The cart horses at the rear heard the tumult and bore away their carts, drivers and all, at full tilt toward the border of Yip, which lay just to the east. But the unlucky war-horses were caught full in the middle of the wolf-pack and were forced to fight their way out of the crush and to flee for their lives.

Nemesis, that great charger, bitten fore and aft, ridden by an unready rider, gave a great horse scream and bolted for freedom. Unfortunately, the stolen sheep had chosen to bolt in the same direction, and soon Nemesis and his royal burden were floating like a chip upon a sea of sheep.

Bewildered by the sudden change in his plans and fortunes, the King spurred his charger forward, trying to outpace his woolly escort and break free. Poor Nemesis was almost as befuddled as his rider, and he shied at the sudden prick in his side, unseating King Grapnel, who fell into a horrible muddle of dust and sheep.

Realizing his mistake, the royal horse struggled back to his master's side and lowered his head so the King could catch his bridle and drag himself upright. Though some dozens of sheep-hooves had stabbed their way across his royal person, the King did so and managed to mount. Then, carefully, he and Nemesis picked their way out of the boiling flock to a bit of high ground.

There he found the regimental bugler, who was wiping the dust from his eyes and trying to count the wolf-bites on his legs. Though his horse was nowhere to be found, he did have his bugle strapped to his shoulder, so the King ordered him to blow an order to assemble.

After a time, what was left of the army managed to find the bugler and the King. They were a sorry-looking group, bitten and battered and dusty. Many were afoot, not having been able to hold their horses. Those still mounted were no better off, as it took all their attention just keeping their steeds from bolting for the mountains.

But King Grapnel was no quitter. Though his schedule was disrupted, he felt that even such an army as this could easily overcome any resistance offered by the militia of I-Wish-It-Would. So he grouped his men as best he could and set off again in the direction of Someday.

As his force drew near to the capitol city, the King saw, to his surprise, that the city gates were closed. Then he seemed to see glints and gleams, as of cannon and armor, between himself and the city walls. And then he could see clearly.

Drawn up in tidy ranks before the gates was a very respectable army, equipped with efficient-looking cannons and highly polished lances. (Though the King didn't know it, quite a bit of this army was on loan from King Robilot of Yip.)

Though he was no quitter, Grapnel was no idiot, either. He knew his weary men and his unnerved horses could never stand up to a fresh and ready army.

Sadly, he motioned his troops to a halt and told the bugler (who was riding behind him on Nemesis) to blow a retreat. He turned his face toward the mountains to the east, for, though they were a part of Yip, he felt that he could travel secretly through their hidden passes to reach the River Olo and home.

But one more terrible surprise awaited him in the mountains. For there the main army of King Robilot, hidden in the trees and the rocky gullies, lay in wait for any move against the borders of Yip. As the remainder of the invading army straggled into the cart-track that led to the passes, King Robilot himself rode out into the way before Grapnel.

"Hold!" he called, and no one laughed, though he looked very small and childish astride his pony, as he confronted the great King on his white charger.

"Twice you have disturbed the peace of your neighbors," he said to King Grapnel. "We do not wish to be troubled again by your country. You shall go with me to Yip City, with all your army, as prisoners. There we will present to you a treaty, which you will sign. And besides that, you will give me your word of honor, as a soldier and a King, that you will never again invade any land.

"Then you shall sit for a year and a day in the Tower of Reason, listening to the teachings of the wise men of Yip. If, at the end of your teachings, you have learned the ways of peace, you will be allowed to go home. If you have not..."—and Robilot looked very stern—"...You will sit for another year and hear it all over again."

So the Prime Minister led the army home to I-Wonder-When, after the signing of the treaty. And, since King

Grapnel sat through several years of teaching in the Tower of Reason and did not learn the ways of peace, the Prime Minister was given permanent control of the government and the army.

King Grapnel was given power to open all the documents first (though he could not sign them). He could ride at the head of the army on days of celebration, and he could proclaim holidays and open all the fairs.

He was also allowed to be the chief patron of all the country's zoos, but, for some reason, he never again cared to look at any animal except Nemesis, and even that seemed to make him unhappy.

ABOUT THE AUTHOR

The author of seventy books, more than forty of them published commercially, **ARDATH MAYHAR** began her career in the early eighties with science fiction novels from Doubleday and TSR. Atheneum published several of her young adult and children's novels. Changing focus, she wrote westerns (as **Frank Cannon**) and mountain man novels (as **John Killdeer**), four prehistoric Indian books under her own name, and historical western *High Mountain Winter* under the byline **Frances Hurst**.

Recently she has been working with on-line publishers. *A Road of Stars* was her first original novel to appear in print-on-demand format. Many of her out-of-print titles are now available from e-publishers fictionwise.com and renebooks.com; many other novels are being published by the Borgo Press Imprint of Wildside Press and Amazon.com.

Now in her eighties, Mayhar was widowed in 1999, after forty-one years of marriage, and has four grown sons. She now works at home, writing short fiction and nonfiction, and doing book doctoring professionally. Her web pages can be found at:

w2.netdot.com/ardathm/

and

http://ofearna.us/books/mayhar.html

THE LOQUAT EYES, BY ARDATH MAYHAR * 163

www.ingramcontent.com/pod-product-compliance
Lightning Source LLC
Chambersburg PA
CBHW020646180626
46816CB00003B/1138